I0782329

TAYLOR PAINTER

The *Primrose* of Bascomb

By Taylor Painter

Published by Forget Me Not Romances, an imprint of Winged Publications

ISBN-13: 978-1-965352-40-3

'Awakening"

1

1 JOHN 5:12

Today has been a heck of a day. One of those where I can't wait to pop a cold one and sink into a hot tub of Epsom salt water. And by cold one, I mean a Coconut *La Croix* with lime, freshly squeezed please.

I'm off tomorrow, praise the Lord. Thirty more minutes left of the shift, if nothing happens. (Knocking on wood.) And oh, the chaos that's capable of unfolding in thirty minutes' time, or even in thirty seconds' time. Of this, I'm certain. But that's just the way the cookie crumbles when you choose the nursing profession.

For as long as I can remember, I'd wanted to be a nurse. It was my dream career and my strong desire to help people, though not necessarily in the way that I just helped the patient in room 108 with a soap suds enema. No, that's not exactly what I had envisioned, but such things go with the territory.

Since I was a little girl, I've had the immense pull to nurture. I can remember several times throughout my childhood years when I'd rescued tiny, pitifully ugly baby birds that'd fallen from their nests, too weak to even hold their acorn-sized heads up. With my father's abundant wisdom, and Grandmama's lap to sit on, I nursed them to health, feeding them farm-fresh egg yolks with a medicine syringe. When they finally became strong and healthy, ready to take flight, I took such pride in setting them free and watching them spread their fully feathered wings for the first time.

They'd jet quickly to the nearest fencepost or tree branch. They'd turn their little heads back and forth, looking around the place where they were born to thrive, as if to say… "My, it sure is big out here."

I imagine they'd forgotten the feel of a cool and subtle breeze, or the sound of other birds singing their morning songs. After several seconds of perhaps just taking in the wonderful new scene before him, natural instinct kicked in and the bird would finally take off. Soaring above the trees, it was free at last. Never again would he consume or wish for the raw eggs or pulverized *Purina Dog Chow* that had sustained him up until then.

It wasn't only birds, but most often it was. I once found a newborn baby squirrel, without a single tuft of fur on its soft, pink body. I somehow managed to save it and keep it alive by force-feeding it sugar water until Daddy was able to get in touch with a *real* wildlife rehabilitator. But no matter what, or who it was, I loved the feeling that came with making another creature better. I had given it strength by providing nourishment and care at a critical time. I'd nurtured it with my own hands. It was something I found great comfort and satisfaction in.

Back then, one might've expected that I'd grow up to choose a career involving wildlife. It started with the baby animals, but by the time I was twelve years old, I was skipping off to volunteer at the local hospital, my red and white candy-striper dress pressed and donned. I thought I was someone really important with my laminated, personalized name badge:

Blaire Whitfield, Volunteer.

I launched myself at any opportunity to practice my self-taught nursing skills at home. Anytime my careful inspection revealed so much as a hangnail or a superficial scratch on my Daddy's rough, calloused hands, I was falling all over myself to get the metal first-aid box from beneath our kitchen sink behind the mint green curtain that Grandmama had sewn. A generous amount of Bag Balm would do the trick and it went on *everything*, from a winter wind-chapped cheek to a blister rubbed from a set of post-hole diggers. Daddy would sit in his easy chair after a long day of farming and let me tend to him whether he needed it or not, Grandmama shaking her head and chuckling under her breath while standing over the stove or sink.

Truthfully, my amateur nursing was probably more of a nuisance than anything else, but Daddy let me do it anyway and he even smiled throughout the duration. "Thank you, darlin," he'd say as I left him slathered in yellow goo and smelling like diesel fuel. It was especially exciting when Daddy needed a bandage that I'd insist on changing every time he washed his hands or bathed. And he was always sure to let me know how nice his injuries were healing up, thanks to my "doctorin".

So, I guess it really came as no surprise to anyone when I decided to go to nursing school right after I graduated from high school. I went to the community college on the other end of Weatherford, making the commute there and back home, daily.

That was seven years ago, before Daddy suffered a debilitating stroke and passed away shortly after, leaving me here…a heartbroken orphan with nothing to call mine except a fifty-five-pound goldendoodle. It was before they took our farm as payment for the six-week-long hospital stay with futile therapies, equipment, and medications. Back when I was an eager nursing student, bursting with excitement for the future.

I do truly enjoy caring for my patients. They bring me bits of joy that I've failed to find otherwise. I still feel the rich satisfaction I felt as a little girl taking care of baby animals or Daddy's cuts and scrapes, when I know I've helped one of my patients to heal. Or in the geriatric field that I've chosen, to at least *feel* better. To feel comforted and cared for, and to bring quality to their days though the quantity may be rapidly dwindling.

Most days, though, it feels more like my patients are just boxes I must check as I go in and out of their rooms at twice the speed of light. Another patient, another suitcase-full of pills for them to hurry up and swallow so I can scurry back to the medicine cart, hurl the empty plastic medicine cup into the trash can attached to the side of my cart, and sprint to the next patient who is anxiously awaiting their suitcase-full of pills.

And this is a large part of why I'm a twenty-seven-year-old disgruntled orphan with depression and peptic ulcers. Oh, let's not forget that I'm single, as I have been for basically my entire life(if you don't count the random hookups in high school, for which shame is included in the list of emotions that course through my being daily.)

"Rough day?" a familiar voice freezes my depressing thoughts. I must've been in a dazed state of exhaustion from this monster of a day, the faint beeping of an IV pump lulling me into my trance. My chin resting on my palm, I realize my eyes have been fixed on the Wong-Baker pain scale posted on the wall-papered wall of the nurses' station.

"Jill!" I exclaim. "I don't think I've ever been more excited to see you!"

"I'll take that as a yes, then?" Jill laughs, placing her oversized Duluth Trading lunch tote on the small table by the door. A no-no, (according to the *Occupational Safety and Health Administration*) but all of the "front office" staff are gone for the day.

"Huh?" I ask, confused but too tired to genuinely care.

"Blaire, you okay? Rough day?" She does genuinely care, and not just because my rough day likely means her rough night as well. She's a wonderful nurse but an even better friend. Jill and I met in nursing school and have been as thick as thieves ever since we practiced vital signs on each other for our nursing skills check-offs, rode together all the way up Queen's Mountain for sixteen-hour clinical rotations, and pulled all-nighters studying for exams that we only passed by the skin of our teeth.

We took our state board exams on the same day, and both passed them that day, though we didn't know it until we received the results in the mail two weeks later. It was a glorious day when we received our letters that we'd finally become nurses, able to reap the fruits of our labor, at last.

Jill and I were even hired here at Sunny Meadows Home & Rehab on the same day, almost five years ago. We came in together, freshly licensed and just hoping to pick up an application to proudly fill out, when we learned that they were in desperate need of nurses and they hired us both, without experience or a single reference. We were ecstatic. Like little schoolgirls giggling with excitement, we hurried to the nearest uniform store and tried on truckloads of scrubs in the colors the nursing home had given us to choose from: black, white, lilac, or coral sunset. We each left with two bags full of brand-new work clothes in black, white, lilac, *and* coral sunset; the buttery soft ones, the ones with cargo pants, the ones with elastic at the ankles. I mean, how could we possibly choose just one style? Of course, we had to have lab jackets to match each outfit too, right? The credit card company made their ten percent interest off each of us that day.

And, of course Jill was there for me when Daddy died. She took time off work from her fairly new job here at Sunny Meadows just so she could be with me while I sat and sobbed uncontrollably for days on end. She knew there was nothing she could do to lessen the stinging pain and despair, but she still came. She came over every day for at least a week, bringing boxes full of doughnuts, milkshakes, and my favorite: Spicy Deluxe Chick-Fil-A sandwiches, complete with *extra* honey mustard and a large lemonade. I appreciated it all very much, though my waistline didn't and I'm sure all of my body's systems were taxed almost as much as my broken heart.

"The Home" as I sometimes call Sunny Meadows, is a quaint and cozy type of facility. Of course, the structure is typical and there are regulations and certain requirements that have to be met to bring the building up to code, but as a whole, the interior has an inviting sort of atmosphere. Most of the nursing staff enter through the single door directly into the homey nurses' station. The small, carpeted room, and most others in the facility have an outdated Victorian-style sort of vibe. Except, maybe adustier, knock-off version.

Carved wooden picture frames filled with various flower paintings and doctors from the antebellum era embellish walls throughout The Home. The dining room is complete with large cherrywood tables and long cotton drapes embroidered with outdated prints. The floors in the dining room and living room are covered with linoleum, though the long hallways that house the residents' rooms are the slick tiles typical of a hospital setting. The kind that patients taking blood thinners fall and bump their heads on.

Decorative candle sconces with small electric bulbs attached to them line the halls, dining room, and nurses' station, though the hallwayshave the addition of fluorescent lights overhead.

The beeping sound of a call bell comes through the speaker in the nurses' station, and my attention resurfaces and tunes into the present situation.

"Girl..." Is all I have to say, eyes wide, and Jill knows.

"How I got finished on time today, I have no idea," I continue as I swivel in the wobbly office chair. "I ate a piece of dried mango for lunch, and I just peed for the first time since 5 am." I squint my eyes and give my best fake smile from my cushioned seat by the exterior door.

I am amazed that I don't have to leave anything for Jill to finish tonight. It causes me stress to leave any of my work for the next shift, but management has really cracked down on overtime. Our last in-service meeting was mandatory for all staff members to attend and it consisted of specific instructions to clock in and out at the exact times in which our shifts begin and end, with a four-minute grace period. If we aren't finished with all tasks at the end of our shift, we must simply pass it to the nursing staff taking our place. That is extremely difficult for me to do. I've had to do it a handful of times since our in-service meeting, and I always leave feeling like I've just set a bomb and I'm slyly dipping out before it blows. All staff members don't share those feelings with me, and it's been made evident when I clock in at 7 am (sometimes, 7:04) and the nightshift nurse is at the desk on her rear end. Not because she's finished all her duties, and the patients are happy and cared for, but instead she's waiting for someone to arrive and take over what she didn't "get to".

Shift report will be a long one today, and I'll be slightly past 19:04 clocking out, but so be it. From two new admissions, to the patient I sent over to the emergency room via ambulance for a suspected exacerbation of congestive heart failure, to the patient I've started on IV antibiotics for an infected wound (that could have totally been avoided). However, I'm not the surgeon who performed the knee replacement surgery, so what do I know? I mentioned the elevation in temperature from baseline two days ago. The on-call doctor (probably a sleep deprived new graduate, being hazed with on-call duties for five days straight) told me to give the patient some Tylenol. That was it. Just "give 1,000 mg Tylenol by mouth." I then reported increased knee pain and excessive drainage on the wound dressing.

"Give an extra pain pill as needed every four hours. Monitor site."

Today, I called an on-call physician with the same knee patient's abnormal lab results, and I reported low blood pressure, diaphoresis, a weak and thready pulse, lethargy.

"The patient is septic. Start one gram Vancomycin IV at 50 ML/hour...."

It's a good thing her kidney function was okay, because he didn't bother to ask.

Once I've reported all the events of the exhausting day to Jill, we've counted all the pills in the jammed-packed narcotics drawer and contemplated our life choices together, I finally hit the time clock at 7:21 pm and exhale the day's weight into the sterile air around me. Our wing is chocked-full of high-maintenance, acutely sick patients right now, but I know if anyone can handle it, Jill can.

The patients on the 100-wing are in good hands tonight. With my giant *Thirty-One* sack hanging from my tight shoulder, I make the short trip around the corner to the time clock and then back through the small nurses' station where I habitually punch in the code to release the heavy door.

"Bye," Jill says as I push the door open.

"Call me later," I reply as I exit the nurses' station and step out onto the tiny deck of a stair landing. Making sure the door shuts behind me to avoid the alarm sounding, I deeply inhale the first breath of fresh air as I stomp down the spiral wooden staircase.

I walk slowly to my car in the serenity of the balmy evening, unhurried for the first time since I opened my eyes this morning. I can almost hear Jill pouring Goody's powders onto her tongue and then washing it down with an ice-cold fizzy flow of Sundrop. It must burn like fire, but she's unfazed.

The night air is warm and soothing after being cooped up indoors for the past twelve hours. The crickets are already singing their night songs; the late summer magnolias' sweet aroma is a nice contrast to some of the odors my nostrils and olfactory nerves have been assaulted with today. The blood orange sun is aglow as it slowly sinks behind the *Sunny Meadows* rooftop, chaos sure to unfold within those brick walls.

Driving home, I roll the windows down and crank up the radio. If I sit still for the twenty-minute drive home without some stimulation, I'm liable to fall asleep at the wheel. As Shania Twain belts out a number about feeling like a woman, I'm feeling like a zombie. Three twelve-hour shifts on the 100-wing of *Sunny Meadows* will wear you out. Although the biggest part of the day is spent on my feet, walking and occasionally running, the mental exhaustion far surpasses the physical.

A few more miles and I'll be home, at last. Though the place I call home is certainly subpar. From the ancient and tattered roof that leaks, to sheets of the siding falling off the house, to dealing with Jason, the hateful landlord for the past half-decade, I am beyond anxious to move out. And, it won't be long now.

Just a few weeks ago, my offer on a house was accepted. Not just any house, but the most wonderful house I could've possibly found. It's the one thing in my life that I'm actually looking forward to.

The reason the home is so perfect isn't the fact that it's a beautifully-aged white farmhouse with a picket fence surrounding flower beds of electric blue hydrangeas and sweetly fragrant gardenias with their velvety white petals and heavenly tropical scent. It's not the charming, covered porch or the weathered tin roof that, in the Fall, is sure to bear the pelting of acorns from the white oak tree standing at the northeast corner of the towering farmhouse.

The house is perfect because it bears such a resemblance to my childhood home. With its three doghouse-style dormers, chippy white porch swing, and simply carved wooden corbels hugging the hand-turned porch posts, I compare the farmhouse I grew up in to the home of *The Waltons*. Only without the sawmill out back. Or the lovely family of eleven.

The new place includes a pasture full of lush, green grass, a small white barn complete with a rooster adorned weathervane on top, and an oddly charming old smokehouse out back. Not that I'm likely to ever use that, but it does really complete the whole nostalgic vibe.

Though I didn't know it then, the fresh years of my childhood and adolescence were the best years I'd ever experience. I spent many summer hours lying on our old sun-beaten porch, coloring pictures, or writing notes to whomever happened to be my best friend at the time.

Grandmama, my Daddy's mother, lived with us as I was growing up and helped to look after me. I'll always remember her in her pink-and-green plaid apron she always wore, with her little brown lace-up shoes and knee-high stockings. She was a jolly lady, short and a bit plump, with short white hair and thick black glasses. She never let any dust settle on her, as Daddy used to say. I guess he got his work ethic honestly. Grandmama was up before daylight every morning to cook our breakfast. She especially loved making homemade flapjacks, and we loved when she made them, too. I know Daddy would've been lost without her stepping in and taking over after my mother died when I was just a baby.

Grandmama would often send me out into the field with a jug of cold drinking water for Daddy. Sometimes, she'd let me ring the dinner bell hanging from the porch rafter once she'd finished preparing a home-cooked meal. Once in a while, she'd let me sit up on the kitchen counter and help chop vegetables or simply watch her. My favorite was when she would soak our home-grown collard greens in a sink full of water. I could help rinse the little dead bugs off after the greens had sat in the water for a while. These are simple little snippets of memories that are deeply ingrained within my soul.

She sure was a special part of our little family up until she passed away of old age during my junior year of high school. Daddy and I were sad and a bit lonesome for a time afterwards. But we managed to get along fine, just the two of us.

My daddy had the biggest crop of vegetables of anyone for miles around. We sold beef and pork that we'd raised, and we had numerous loyal customers that'd come out to our farm just to buy our chickens' eggs. We, too, had a little smokehouse out back where we smoked many cuts of beef and pork. I suppose that's why I feel a bit of comfort when I look at the old abandoned shack I'm now the owner of. I can almost see Grandmama slicing a slab of smoked bacon she'd traveled out to the old smokehouse to retrieve when it had finished curing.

I loved when Daddy would invite me to help him on the farm. He always welcomed me patiently when I ventured out to watch him working, or to ask him a dozen questions. And when he took it upon himself to ask for my assistance with something, it felt like the ultimate treat, next to being able to cure a wound. Daddy was so gentle and kind. The only time I ever heard him raise his voice was when he was chasing an escapee hog.

I'm confident I was the only kid at school in the 1990's who had ever taken part in butchering a chicken or a pig, could operate a tractor, or had spent considerable time digging up potatoes. Daddy was country and he was old-fashioned, but I loved that about him. I loved everything about him.

Pulling onto my narrow pea-gravel driveway and facing the small beige cracker box of a house, I wonder what Dill is doing inside. I'm sure he's standing at the front door, wagging his feather duster of a tail at the sound of the garage door opening. The moment I step inside, he will stand on his hind feet with his front paws on my shoulders and he'll repeatedly lick each of my cheeks with the ferocious swipe of his enormous slobbery tongue. I have to admit, it feels nice to be loved. I don't know anybody else in the entire world that would be willing to lick nursing home off of my face.

Though he's a giant now, I've had him since he was a ten-week-old ball of butter-colored fluff. I was pleasantly surprised when the butthead landlord agreed to let me have a pet. I'll bet he's dying to pee. Dill, that is.

I'm almost bowled over by his enthusiastic greeting. "Goodness boy, did you miss me? I missed you too. Yes, Mama missed her boy," I promise as I scratch his ears and kiss his warm, soft muzzle. I finally manage to break free of his embrace so that I can relieve myself of my heavy bag and retrieve his leash.

"Come on. Go potty?" I ask, as if it's a real question. Dill leaps at his leash before I can even take it from its hook by the door.

Once Dill and I have taken a quick trip outside and are safely back inside, I lock the deadbolt and treat him to his long-awaited Milk Bone.

"Here, one more," I offer before I put the cardboard box back into the kitchen cupboard and reach for the refrigerator door. My favorite drink is waiting for me on the top shelf in all its shiny aluminum glory. I grab it along with a pre-sliced lime wedge and combine the two over the gloriously satisfying pebble-shaped ice from my beloved countertop ice maker.

With my large cup in hand, I shuffle the mere twenty feet down the cream-colored shag carpeted hallway and into my bedroom where I utilize the stained drink coaster on my vanity. I undress, taking care not to swipe my germy scrub top over my lips. There's no telling of the things that could have possibly come into contact with the fibers of my uniforms today.

Once I've filled the tub with nearly scalding water and I've added a heaping cup of epsom salt to it, I make sure the door is cracked for Dill before lowering myself into the steamy lava that consumes my overtired body and consoles my tight, rigid muscles. Sometimes, especially when I've been away all day, Dill likes to sit next to the bathtub and keep me company while I bathe. He also sometimes likes to lean over the edge of the tub and lap my dirty body-water, as if he doesn't have a clean bowl of filtered water in the kitchen. It's gross, but on the other hand, I've never, and surely never will, have another male adore me enough to drink my bathwater.

After a refreshing sip of the icy coconut lime concoction, I lean back and rest my head on the cold, outdated seafoam green tiles and allow my heavy eyelids to close. I could easily go to sleep right here. But I find my mind wandering over to the sweet thoughts of my soon-to-be new (though actually old) farmhouse. The one thing that can (almost) put Blaire Whitfield in a good mood.

I find myself smiling at the image of the farmhouse, adorned with waxy emerald ivy crawling across the front banister, and a genuine twisted metal lightning rod on top of the house. I can imagine my younger self swaying on the front porch swing, cradling some sort of lame infant creature. Holding it in a small blanket like it was my own newborn baby. Not longing for anyone or anything else; just completely satisfied with the air I breathed.

My future home in the country will be in Bascomb County and is about ten miles away. I've lived here in Weatherford my entire life. It's where I went to school, where my job is, where I've always called home. In fact, I've never even traveled outside of the state of North Carolina.

My childhood home, now occupied by complete strangers, is only four miles from my rental. But I can't bear to see it again, at the end of the winding country road where it sits nestled in a grove of robust red maples. The last time I saw the old house was the day I had to help move Daddy's things out of it while he slowly slipped away, from the bed of a sterile hospital room. It was one of the saddest days I've encountered, second to losing Daddy shortly after selling the house and land that we'd farmed together. Gone, like it wasn't our home and livelihood for all those precious years.

Today is September 13th. I've dated enough documents and wound dressings today to know. That means it's been seven days since I closed on the loan. I had been saving every bit I possibly could and was able to apply a decent down payment on the house, so I will only owe around $100,000. That amount doesn't seem like too much to me, but my Daddy would roll over in his grave at the thought of owing that kind of money. As far as I know, he never owed anyone so much as a stick of gum. He just didn't believe in borrowing, and he tried to teach me the same rule of thumb. If I'd been smarter, I would have listened to his words of wisdom, and I wouldn't have any debt at all. But I'll admit I have been influenced by today's world where folks just run up a hefty bill for the things they can't actually afford. I've done pretty well for myself though, so I guess Daddy's attempts at preparing me for successful adulthood weren't in vain. All my credit cards currently have a zero balance, and my vehicle is paid for, so the only debt I will have will be the mortgage loan. And it will be well worth any interest, guilt, or stress I may suffer.

The whole process has gone very smoothly, and I'm hoping to be able to move in within the next few weeks. The current owners are moving to another state. Mississippi, I believe they said. They seem like a sweet enough family of four and have been pleasant to do business with.

Apparently, they only lived in the house for ten months before deciding to move away. The dad's job or something. Either way, I sure am glad they're passing the place to me to nestle into and add my own touches that'll make it a comfortable home for me and Dill.

I think I'll drive up to *Bobbies's Antiques* tomorrow. I'm always able to find great pieces there, and I'm on the hunt for a couple of large stoneware crocks which I can visualize containing scarlet chrysanthemums on my new front porch in the fall.

TWO

EPHESIANS 6:12

Bobbie's looks like a popular place on this warm, sunny morning. It almost always is though, and it's no wonder. Located at the foot of the mountains and right beside a busy interstate, it's a charming two-story old homeplace, now full of treasures waiting to be re-homed. Blooming Crepe Myrtle trees surround the parking lot, their deep purple, magenta, and white blossoms like tufts of fragrant Hawaiian leis placed on the velvety branches.

I spot a silver Subaru with reverse lights aglow, so I wait. And wait. Finally, they realize I want the (only available) spot and very slowly back out. That took way longer than it should've but I've managed to park my car at last.

Inside, the store is humming with a vibrant bustle. Shoppers meandering across the creaky hardwood floors, slowly browsing the eclectic variety of things Bobbie, the owner and ultimate "picker" has sought out and placed here. The cha-ching of the cash register plays in unison with the fiddles and banjos in the background. If I know Bobbie, it's probably an old bluegrass CD, or maybe even a cassette tape. The store smells of fresh apple cobbler while the orange flame of a candle flickers on the oak counter by the cash register. It feels like the walls of the long-retired home, decked with rusty lanterns and percolators and washboards, are embracing you in a welcoming hug. Ordinarily, I reject all types of affection from anyone or anything but Dill. But, I'm almost tempted to succumb to the fuzzy feeling that tries to overtake me as I take a step back in time.

As usual, I help myself to a piece of the free peanut brittle offered to shoppers, from the basket in the hands of a three-foot cloth Aunt Jemima doll. Then, I begin to slowly wander over the first floor, with the wide scuffed boards creaking and popping beneath my feet as I scan the vintage merchandise before me.

If I were a large crock, where would I be? I wonder. The shop is jam-packed with so many primitive treasures, from the floor to the ceiling. I could scavenge all day and still not see everything. I haven't seen Bobbie yet, but I know she's here someplace. Probably in a corner with a cleaning rag in her hand, dusting some of the less popular pieces of glassware that have been sitting awhile.

It doesn't take me long to start gathering things I find along the way, but I've yet to find what I came in search of. After exploring every square inch of the downstairs portion, I make my way over to the staircase in the middle of the floor - what I assume was once a living room. Looking up the glossy pine staircase with my arms filled with old cocoa tins, a pair of candlesticks, and a blue checkered tablecloth, I halfway hope I don't find what I'm looking for up there. If I were to find a giant, heavy stoneware crock, I imagine it would be difficult to get it back downstairs. I make the trek up the stairs anyway, for I can't resist the urge to see what might await.

On the second floor, I discover there are just as many fellow pickers picking as there were downstairs. The sweet, spicy aroma of the candle burning accompanies me as I carefully weave around other shoppers, bits of shattered peanut brittle snapping beneath my Birkenstocks.

Right away, my eyes land on it and I halt in my sugary dust tracks. Sort of tucked away among an assortment of Vaseline glass oil lamps and large butter churns, it beckons me. I make a beeline for it against the shelf-lined beadboard wall, to find that it's even more beautiful up close. A glimpse of someone passes by in front of me, but I'm too engaged to even acknowledge them.

Kneeling to get level with it, I run my free hand along the smooth top. It's quite dusty, I notice. I can't imagine this beautiful piece sitting here for very long without being snatched up. I rock it back and forth a little to find that it's very sturdy and nicely built. This is not a Hobby Lobby massed-repro; someone built this with their hands and pieced it together with wooden pegs, seemingly many years ago. The little table has been painted white, which has slowly chipped away naturally and beautifully. It has long, spindly tapered legs, and a single shallow drawer adorned with a beautiful, amber-colored glass knob.

I attempt to open the drawer, but I lose my balance and nearly fall right onto the floor as I realize the drawer is stuck. Steadying myself, I adjust the items cradled in my left arm, and make another weak attempt because truthfully, the table is going home with me whether the drawer will open or not. Surely a piece this old wouldn't have been made with a faux drawer, right? Functionality would have been of utmost importance I would assume. On the other hand, the tabletop will hold midnight snacks just fine, regardless of the drawer's function.

I can see that the drawer *does* open, or at least it has been able to in the past, as I make an opening no more than a half inch. Wriggling the drawer up and down as best I can with one arm, a shriek escapes the lovely dame.

Finally, I place the items I've been carrying on the hardwood floor. I hug the table with my left arm and grasping the stunning little drawer-pull with my right hand, I make another attempt. I try yanking the drawer but it's too tight inside the frame of the table, almost like the wood has swelled at some point. I decide to slam the drawer shut for now. I can work with it some more at home; it's simply too beautiful to pass by.

Like nails on a chalkboard, it screeches and then loudly claps as the two parts meet again. Slowly turning it around and inspecting it on all sides, I locate the price tag taped to the back - a piece of paper with "Nightstand $10" written on it in Bobbie's feminine cursive scribble.

Taking the tag, I hurriedly stuff it amongst the other items I intend to purchase and make a quick lap around the remainder of the upstairs area to be sure there's nothing else I can't live without.

After seeing none, I rush downstairs to find Bobbie behind the counter busily cleaning the window that looks out onto the front porch of the store.

"Hey, Mrs. Bobbie!" I greet her.

She looks over her shoulder, brows furrowed below her wispy salt and pepper bangs. The curious look of puzzlement is instantly replaced by a broad smile when she recognizes me, arms full of merchandise, as usual.

"Hey, honey!" Bobbie returns the greeting enthusiastically with the wave of her cleaning rag, before tossing it onto the counter. Dusting her hands on her blue jeans as she approaches the cash register.

I step up to the store counter and relieve myself of the armful of loot upon it.

"I'll take this stuff out to my car and come back for *this* little beauty," I tell Bobbie with a sly grin as I slide the price tag across the counter.

"What in the world did you find today?" Bobbie asks, extending her arm and holding the paper tag as far away as possible to accommodate her far-sightedness.

"I've lost my glasses again, go figure!" she laughs.

"Nightstand ten dollars," she finally reads aloud.

"Oh…" Bobbie draws out. "Is this that white table upstairs with the little brown glass knob?" She doesn't wait for my reply.

"You know what, darlin? The only reason I remember it right now is because I was up there earlier today helping a nice gentleman, and I stumped my pinky toe on the leg of that little cuss! It is sturdy, I tell you. It didn't budge an inch! Darn near broke my toe in two!" Bobbie declares.

I stifle a laugh at her typical Bobbie quip.

"Oh goodness, Mrs. Bobbie. I'm sorry about that! How long has it been hiding up there, anyway?" I ask in an attempt to will my thoughts from the image of Bobbie tripping and cursing over the beautiful and blameless table.

"Well, as I recall….", she chews on her lip. "I picked it up at a thrift store," Bobbie recollects, seemingly still unsure.

"I betcha it's been up there for six months and ain't a single person taken a liking to it before now, I declare! Well, I should have left it down here instead of lugging it up them blame steps, knowing good and well nobody would have the gumption to carry it back down. Well, nobody but *Blaire* of course! I might've known!" she guffaws.

I suppose it *has* been awhile since I've shopped here, so that might explain why I haven't seen it before.

"I just *love* it!" I reply. "It will be perfect by my bed to hold books and my phone at night." I don't mention the snacks.

"You younguns and your phones, I declare! What in the world would you do without them?" Bobbie asks.

"I'd be late for work, that's what! My phone wakes me up whenever I tell it to, Mrs. Bobbie. Do you believe that?" I can't help but reciprocate her teasing just a little bit, but only because I know it'll make her laugh. Which it does, very much.

Once she's gathered herself and rang me up with the help of her dark-rimmed bifocals she has found in the cash drawer, she offers to help me carry the things to my car which I politely decline but tell her she can help me with the nightstand if she doesn't mind. She agrees, of course and to my relief. I wasn't especially looking forward to wrestling with it while meeting unprepared patrons mid-flight of stairs.

"Isn't it the cutest?" I ask once we've climbed the stairs.

"The drawer didn't want to open very easily, but I'll work on it," I say as we hoist the table up and start toward the staircase in a three-legged-race type of gait.

"Well, I'm glad you've taken a liking to this thing, honey, and I hope you enjoy it," Bobbie comments, slightly short of breath as the three of us inch down the stairs. "I'm sure it will look real nice in your new home. Me, I wouldn't give two red cents for it."

Bobbie doesn't crack a smile as she mumbles insults at my new bedside table.

"You need to work on your sales pitch, or I just might have to ask for a refund on this old thing," I kid.

"Oh, I'm just teasing, old lady!" Bobbie chortles as we inch down the steep stairs.

Once outside, we side shuffle across the pavement toward my Camry, in the homestretch now. The late morning sun is already beginning to turn the parking lot into a griddle, and the dew drops that clung to the manicured blades of grass around it have now burned off. Although it's technically only a week until the first day of fall, our southern state of North Carolina won't feel that first crisp promise of autumn for several more weeks. I don't rush it, though. Summer has always been my most favorite season, when the long, leisurely days are dripping with a sweet southern heat, as slowly as the people are sauntering about.

I'm happiest when my skin is dewy, golden tan, and smelling of coconut. Gorging myself on a big bowl of fresh fruit or Old Bay seasoned shrimp or snow cones, searching for seashells on a vacant beach, living barefooted with stacks of ankle bracelets on each ankle, and watching fireworks are all things that give me a glimmer of life.

I don't make it to the beach as often as I would like to - mainly because it's a four-hour trip to the coast, but wherever I am, I much prefer Carolina summers to the bitter cold, dead days of winter.

"Whew! That got me winded!" Bobbie puffs, once we've laid the table among the assortment of first aid supplies scattered about in the trunk of my car. She steps backward and wipes her brow with the back of her hand.

"Thank you so much, Mrs. Bobbie. That was tough, getting it all the way down here." I softly drum the drawer of the table with my fingertips.

"Wasn't one bit of trouble, honey," she assures me, still slightly short of breath. "Did me some good to get some exercise. And thank you for taking the dusty old thing off my hands!" Bobbie laughs with her mouth wide open and claps her hands together.

Oh, to have her delightful spirit must feel so light and merry.

Closing the door on today's treasures, I thank Bobbie again for her help and reluctantly accept one of her boisterous embraces that I receive every time I visit. I adore Mrs. Bobbie and I have since the first time I met her, but being hugged is one of those things that just makes me want to scream for help. I refrain, however.

Driving home with the golden sun warm on my face, I feel satisfied with today's finds. The table in particular, of course. I can already see it standing next to the four-poster bed in my new bedroom. The evening sun will illuminate the glass honey-colored knob, making it glow.

Daydreaming about my new home decor almost causes me to miss my Chick-fil-A exit and that would be a near tragedy. Thankfully, there's nobody in the right lane and I'm able to scoot over just in time to make the exit for my beloved chicken sandwich. The peanut brittle has worn off long ago.

Once I'm home and fed, maybe I'll unload the antiques I bought, pack them up for the move and then just settle in with a box of French Toast Crunch for dessert in front of The First 48. I probably shouldn't watch such shows; it does make me kind of paranoid sometimes, but it is among the few things I enjoy.

As usual, Dill greets me most enthusiastically as soon as I've stepped through the front door.

"Goodness, boy. I've only been gone a little while!" I say as I scratch his ears.

"Alright, get down," I playfully command. "Mama found some good stuff today that I have to unload," I inform him, never doubting he knows exactly what I'm talking about.

I begin bringing in the loot from the car, to pack away in my moving boxes. No point in using any of them now; I'll have to pack them up to move soon anyway. I start with the small things and leave the table for last. I think I'll dust it with a wet rag and wrap it in an old sheet for the move.

Although it's not very large, it's a lot heavier when you don't have help, I realize as I heave the nightstand up and over the threshold of the front door. Luckily it was just a short trip from the trunk of my car where I've backed into the garage, to the door, with just the one step to hurdle.

As I sit the table down on the kitchen floor, I suddenly hear something. I'm not sure how Bobbie and I both failed to notice it earlier, but it sounds like there's something sliding around inside that pesky drawer. The table becomes even more interesting.

Planting myself on the floor with the table, I roll up the sleeves of my sweatshirt in preparation to really man-handle this piece of furniture.

"Alright," I begin to gently scold. "You're gonna have to let me have this drawer, do you hear?" Hugging the table, I use some muscle power with my strongest arm.

It answers with the same screeching nails-on-a-chalkboard sound as earlier as I pry it open no more than two inches.

"This isn't working too well, is it?" I ask aloud.

My attempts seem futile and I realize I'm talking to a piece of furniture.

I decide to push it up against the nearest wall for extra support while I straighten my legs against it and use both hands to pull at the glass knob.

"Come on," I coax. "I bragged on you, you know."

I guess whatever is in here got left behind because no one could get the stupid drawer open to take it out. All I know is it had better not be a flashlight or something equally uninteresting.

Finally, wiggling the drawer up and down, I'm able to make some progress. "Yes, that's it! Just a little bit more, please," I beg, hoping the glass knob doesn't detach.

At last, the drawer reluctantly slides open three or four inches with one last tug. Enough room for me to easily get my hand inside. Only, I'm afraid to. I'm not crazy about reaching my hand into places I can't see.

Standing quickly, I rush to retrieve a flashlight from the drawer by the fridge. Switching it on, I once again lower myself to the floor in front of the table and shine the light into the opening I've broken a sweat to make.

"Don't be a flashlight; I already have one, see? How about a chunk of gold?" Wouldn't that be something, to hit a gold mine with a ten-dollar wooden table? Not likely.

Peering into the drawer, I see the spiral metal of a notebook's spine. Well that's kind of interesting. Not a gold brick, but interesting nonetheless.

Reaching in, I retrieve the small notebook. About an inch thick, the cover is speckled with little pink and yellow flowers, no bigger than dimes. Some are solid pink, while others are lemon yellow with the same shade of pale pink in their centers and bright green foliage blurred into the background.

Turning the floral cardboard cover reveals a page full of elegant cursive handwriting in thin black ink.

Wonderment fills me as I quickly shuffle through the pages like a deck of cards and see that over half of the book is filled with the charming scrawl. Still sitting on the kitchen floor, I flip back to the first page and lean back against the cabinet doors as I read.

THREE
JEREMIAH 1:5

Each day is slightly shorter than the previous one, a subtle change however noticed and welcomed. It's surely becoming the season of autumnal harvest. The chilly, auburn transition of turning inward and settling in for a period of long-awaited rest. It's my very favorite season, and in my opinion, the best one for births. The mothers have had access to fresh summer foods all season past; the light crisp air is a refreshing and delightful contrast to the long days dripping with sweltering heat, yet it's not frigid enough to chill the new mother in the weeks following the childbirth; and the warm foods she will need to nourish her body with are ones that she'll find most appropriate and will want to enjoy. Overwhelming relief will flood the new mother as she sips warm soups and herbal teas while rocking her precious newborn baby, Earthside at last.

This particular autumn is an oddly bittersweet time for me. Sweet, because my heart is full with memories and life experiences that will remain with me until I pass from this world. As I write this, I'm nearing the end of an accomplished career. I'm currently caring for my final patient before my knee operation, which is scheduled at the end of next month. I'm both optimistic and apprehensive, considering I've never had any sort of surgery, but it's now become necessary. Though the pain is rather severe at times and the function and mobility of my left knee is moderately impaired, I've managed to get along with arnica and comfrey salves, turmeric root, and the oil of wintergreen. I suppose a very fulfilling forty years' worth of regularly milking a cow, weeding a garden, and catching babies has taken a toll on my valuable but overused knee joints. I feel strongly that this intervention would have occurred much sooner had it not been for my daily consumption of homemade collagen-rich bone broth.

For my own pleasure and personal therapy, I've kept a diary for many years. Some of my previous ones hold many notable stories from the mind and soul of a seasoned midwife. I believe the small binder displaying the beautiful monarch butterfly as well as the one with the graceful sea turtle on the cover, hold the most remarkable and special contents. I most certainly would have been overwhelmed with emotion as I recorded those accounts which I never want to forget. Those diaries, each filled with my own words from cover to whimsical cover, have been tucked away for safekeeping under the removable floor plank inside the upstairs coat closet. Though there's no one to read them but me, and I'm sure to revisit them, I would never create the possibility of violating the privacy of any of the mothers mentioned in my writings. Madge, my truest and closest friend, will be the one to go through my belongings assuming I depart before her. She will know how to properly dispose of such things to ensure my wishes and the privacy of my patients are both honored.

In regard to this book in my hands, I couldn't resist the impulse to buy it as the cover displays the beautiful evening primrose, a familiar and lovely botanical extractive included in my regime for expectant mothers. A wonderful ripening aid, similar in effect to the sensational borage oil I've used in years past. The notebook itself will undoubtedly be filled with the monotonous recordings of the day-to-day chores and profound thoughts I have as I enter into the retirement phase. Maybe some honest reflection of my enriched life will be recorded here as well.

As of right now though, I'm nursing a warm cup of red rooibos tea with honey and fresh cream that I skimmed from this morning's milking. Ginger, my beloved Jersey cow, graciously gives me a gallon of milk each morning. Because she is no longer feeding her calf, she gladly gives me all of the rich, delicious cream as well. In keeping with true maternal instinct, she would hold back the cream for her baby during the time that I was sharing the milk with the calf. I've since taken the six-month-old steer to another farm just down the road. There, it can graze happily until the day that it will pay the ultimate sacrifice and return to nourish my body, and ordinarily, the bodies of the women I care for as well. I would normally raise the beef myself as there is enough pastured grass to adequately support two animals, and I allow the calf to nurse from Ginger for a full two years. Milk-fed beef is, by far, the most delectable meat I've ever had the pleasure of tasting.

But, with my impending surgery and a patient sure to give birth any day, I figured it best to allow my farmer friends, the Garveys, to take care of the beef for me. He will graze their lush, healthy fields of ryegrass up until his last day. I've also arranged for different members of the Garvey family to take turns milking Ginger, as well as taking over other farm chores, while I recover. She will have to be milked every morning, but the payment of an abundance of fresh milk seemed like more than fair payment in the opinion of my generous fellow farmers who do not keep a dairy cow themselves but enjoy the plethora of benefits from consuming the unpasteurized whole milk.

While enjoying my comforting yet invigorating latte, I'm vigilant, staying by the phone in case AnnaRuth should need me. She has been pregnant for forty-one weeks, as of yesterday. I went out to her home for a weekly visit and delivered my usual offerings to the expectant mother... farm fresh eggs, beef liver, a few jars of homemade broth, a gallon of Ginger's milk, and a replenishment of herbs that I grow especially for the mothers' tea. A delicious medicinal combination of mint, raspberry leaf, alfalfa, dandelion root, and nettle will serve as a powerful nourishing and uterine-toning infusion. The nettles are also very rich in vitamin K, which plays an important part in preventing hemorrhage after the baby is born. More than just an offering, these are things I recommend to my patients as an imperative part of their prenatal care. In this way, as well as the recommendation to consume additional protein and high-quality fats, I am able to almost totally avoid any occurrences of pre-eclampsia, elevated blood sugars or blood pressures, and even morning sickness.

All of which are alarmingly common in the modern obstetric setting.

In addition to my standard recommendations, I have a handful of things I do discourage my patients from taking…teratogens such as antacids, anti-nausea and motion sickness drugs, and even certain herbs like sage, hops, and ginseng. I've yet to deliver a baby with a birth defect and I believe it is, in large part, because my patients generally refrain from consuming these kinds of potentially harmful substances.

This will be AnnaRuth's first child. Her pregnancy has been smooth and uneventful, and I have no reason to suspect that the birth will be any different, although each woman and birth differ from the next in some way. She has shown no signs of impending labor, but the baby must come out and so it will, at the most perfect time. I've encouraged AnnaRuth to try to relax and trust her body, as it knows what to do and exactly when to do it.

Sadly, in our rather comical obstetrics culture today, we're setting women up for failure of a natural birth by molesting them with unnecessary interventions as though we've forgotten how incredible and capable the woman's body is on its own.

Many women opt for an elective cesarean, which I personally consider an oddity. Between the large needle inserted into the spine, the IV tubes, the urinary catheter, the presence and eventually the painful removal of drain tubes from the tender incision, excessive gas from the procedure causing abdominal bulging and pulling at the sutures, and recovery from a major operation while caring for a newborn just does not seem like a convenience, in my opinion.

These operations are necessary at times. But those times in which it is a true necessity are extremely rare. Yet, the occurrence of cesarean sections is shockingly high. Take this common scenario of the greatly flawed system as an example...

A woman is pregnant beyond the date which the physician has deemed her "due date", or she has a preventable elevated blood pressure which he doesn't take the time to try and reduce, and he certainly hasn't educated the mother on how to prevent. So, the mother is given medications in an attempt to start labor artificially. In conjunction with the IV lines hanging from her, the woman is confined to a bed where fetal doppler and blood pressure apparatuses are strapped to her, and she is allowed nothing to eat except ice chips. The fluorescent lights above her head are stimulating her neocortex thus inhibiting the brain stem from producing the hormones needed to relax enough to give birth. An epidural is then placed in her spinal column with medications pushed into it that cause serious side effects for the baby, as well as numbness from the mother's waist down. She therefore needs a urinary catheter placed inside of her as she lies in bed "in labor".

Because she has been lying horizontally without any form of nutrition, her body has weakened so much that if the mother makes it to the pushing phase of labor, then she is too exhausted to push the baby out.

Suddenly, a combination of maternal exhaustion and a plummet in the baby's heart rate as a result of the medications, have created an emergency situation. One of two things will happen: either the mother is cut with scissors and the baby is pulled out by the head using cold metal forceps, or they begin frantically scrubbing the mother for surgery. Before anyone knows what is happening, everyone is rushing around, wheeling mom to the operating room as quickly as possible, while the dad is left clueless and frightened.

Once the baby is pulled from the incision, it is whisked away from its mother first thing for respiratory support. Its little lungs weren't yet developed enough to breathe on its own outside the womb, which is why it needed a little more time inside. What we've done so far is cause two things: fetal distress and emergency cesarean. Oh, but they've "saved" the baby, haven't they? Modern obstetrics are very good at handling emergency situations, I will say that much.

Later, comes the postpartum depression and anxiety for the new mother, in large part because she was not allowed oxytocin or endorphins to rush through her body as she held her newborn immediately to her chest. Her mental state at her postpartum check-up will urge the doctor to prescribe antidepressants which will completely diminish her milk supply that she had been trying so hard to increase and maintain. On top of this traumatic birth experience, she may also suffer permanent damage from the epidural that was gouged into her spine. This is the tip of the iceberg, but a story I've heard more times than I care to count. I call it the "waterfall of interferences".

Women today are made to forget their innate ability to grow a healthy baby and give birth normally and naturally. I'm eternally grateful for the women who recognize the powerful and unique ability of their bodies. Without them, of course, I would not have had the divine pleasure of living out my fulfilling and blissful calling.

Upon feeling AnnaRuth's abdomen yesterday, the baby had descended low into the pelvis and was positively head downward. If the baby was in the breech position, I can only assume I'd deliver him or her just as I have the other thirty-three babies that were born feet - or bottom- first. It would, however, make it a more difficult delivery for the mother. The secret, which can be a tricky one, is in getting the mother to relax so that the cervix does not trap the baby's head inside. Though, I'm not fully convinced that it's likely, or even possible, considering out of the thirty-three breech-presenting babies I've assisted with, none of them have ever "gotten stuck".

Assuming everything goes as planned, upon this final birth I will have delivered one thousand babies. Of those, I've accompanied nine women to the hospital, most of which, after very long labors, were failures to progress due to exhaustion, combined with the woman's informed choice to receive pain medication. Two have resulted in a cesarean section, two more have presented with shoulder dystocia which were both corrected by changing the position of the mother, three were born not breathing, and I've lost none.

I will admit, I would be a bit uneasy attending a birth of which I had not cared for the mother and saw for myself that she had properly cared for herself while growing the baby, creating a non-toxic womb environment. Likewise, I would expect a mother to be skeptical about giving birth in the presence of those who had no experience delivering babies in the natural way, without scalpels, scissors, forceps or any other sharp, cold metal tool at arm's reach.

I've always followed a strict rule of caring for a maximum of three women at one time so that I could devote the best quality of care possible to them. For this reason, I've never publicly promoted my business. Yet, I've been able to maintain an average of two women per month for most of my practice.

By the door and ready to go, is my large "birth bag" full of supplies. Among the assortment of neat little sterile packages and emergency resuscitation equipment, I've also packed a soft cream-colored baby blanket which I always hand-knit as a gift for the new bundle of love; an infusion of echinacea and goldenseal to cleanse the newborn's eyes with; and an assortment of home-grown herbs to help soothe the mother's bottom as she heals.

I am hyper aware that I could receive that phone call at any moment over the next couple of weeks, so I will stay close to home and relish my last few weeks as a practicing midwife. My, how the years have flown. Forty grand ones! Of course, there have been days here and there which were laden with sadness. I stopped grieving over the loss of my loved ones a long time ago, but the twinges of loneliness never seem to fade completely away.

I try to honor my late husband and son with everything I do, although I am sure I fail often. It's hard to believe I've been alone for seventeen years now, since the passing of my beloved Isaiah. He left me, a mournful widow, following a terrible fall from the roof of a barn belonging to his close friend whom he was helping. Isaiah was always the one people called upon for help, and he gladly responded to each request. The void in my heart and soul will remain until I meet my precious mate again.

And then there's the devastation that can only be the result of losing a child, no matter their age. It has to be among the worst pains one can possibly endure. Isaiah struggled right along with me and carried me through the pits of my agonizing despair at the tragedy that took our Michael from us. To think of it now, such a distant yet vivid memory, feels tender and haunting. A day I can suppress, but cannot forget, is the day that four Air Force officers knocked on our front door, navy blue uniforms donned as their faces like stone looked into ours as we processed the grievous news. Michael would have been forty years old this past July 4th, if he hadn't been taken from us during the fatal fighter jet crash that claimed his life and the lives of his fellow airmen: Joseph B. Edwards, David O. Hansen and

Benjamin R. Wallace, the pilot.

My hand will not allow the pen to meet with paper regarding the devastating nightmare which we lived following the death of Michael. I've been there and done that, long ago. And again, when I lost Isaiah. Today, I'm looking forward to delivering one more precious baby into this world that I recognize I'm merely passing through. I embrace that fact and appreciate the necessity of mortality, more strongly in recent years as our culture languishes quickly.

There's still about an hour of daylight left. I had better let Cookie, my calico "barn" cat inside or else she will be sure to let me know through agonizing pleas by the back door. I enjoy her company very much, though. There's something familiar and inviting about a soft, purring cat sleeping on the foot of a neatly made bed. Cookie adds the perfect charm to a dimly lit room, simply by being in it.

Once I let her in for the evening and make myself a bite of supper, I don't plan to do very much else. I guess you can say that I myself have been through the "nesting" phase of pregnancy in synchrony with my patient. Over the last several weeks, I've spent many satisfying hours preserving the last of the summer harvest.

Lining my deep pantry shelves are homemade raspberry and peach jams, tomato sauces, chutneys and relishes, pickled beets, okras, cucumbers, of course, and green tomatoes.

The glass apothecary cabinet holds wide mouthed jars of dried lemon balm, raspberry leaves, elderberries, horehound, fennel, and chamomile, to name a few.

Contained in dark cobalt blue bottles with handwritten labels are strongly infused tinctures of forsythia, coneflowers, cramp bark, mullein, and goldenseal among others.

Herb-infused honeys of sage, thyme, cinnamon sticks, and garlic are beautifully displayed in a neat row, each small jar its own rich shade of amber with appealing bits of the herbs throughout the thick golden nectar.

I've stored the entire potato and onion harvest downstairs in the basement, along with ten gallons of lacto-fermented produce, which are probiotic-rich and super for gut health and in turn, a high-functioning immune system.

Next to my beloved coffee station that I visit each morning without fail, are glass gallon-sized jars that sit on the counter each containing a potent infusion of herbs, roots, and vinegar. This is my "fire cider" brew that will steep over the next two months before serving me as a powerful herbal tonic all winter long. Of course, I always make enough to trade with my dear friend Madge for some of her homemade candles. I always appreciate a source of the soft flickering glow that I find a very comforting addition to a room, particularly in the cold, dark months.

I think that basically sums up the products of the "nesting" that I've been doing as of late. The house is tidy and smells of fragrant thyme and rosemary. A jelly jar on the small dining table holds the last of my cut purple coneflowers from the potager garden. I will appreciate being able to return to a serene and inviting home after the new mother and baby are both settled. I will most likely come home and rest for several hours at that time, before returning with a nourishing meal for AnnaRuth and her husband. I will spend the next few hours cleaning up her home, providing any assistance that I can, and making sure the new mother does absolutely nothing other than sit or lie comfortably and hold her newborn baby. This is not an issue for the vast majority of my patients, as I've previously stressed the importance of her postpartum rest and healing period. The fathers have mostly all been very understanding of this as well.

I think I'll warm a slice of my sourdough bread that I made yesterday, blanket it in divine, golden homemade butter courtesy of Ginger, and serve it alongside some leftover quinoa-kale soup. Not much goes to waste as I enjoy all of the foods I prepare until they're gone. What I don't consume will be turned into compost for my gardens or fed to my laying hens, which they show their gratitude for by laying an abundance of eggs for me, in a variety of beautiful colors. Various shades of blue, brown, and cream eggs overflow my wire basket by the stove, their shells covered in nature's "bloom" left by the hens to preserve the eggs. When left undisturbed, the waxy bloom will protect the eggs from spoilage for at least two months at room temperature. They never hang around that long in my house, however! Between myself and the mothers I care for, we go through the fresh eggs at a swift pace.

I assume I'll slowly decompress this evening and prepare to rise early tomorrow morning. I'll need to milk Ginger before going into town for a few kitchen staples. That is, if I have not heard from AnnaRuth.

Aside from the therapeutic effects I've already mentioned, I surmise the reason I'm recording these intricate, intimate details of my life are for my own personal validity. Perhaps in the quiet, still moments of my otherwise pleasantly active life, I feel a bit unseen. If only by the blank white pages of a flower-speckled notebook, I feel acknowledged in the depths of my empty nest. Though it may seem like an absurd sign of insecurity, I truly don't feel I'm any weaker of a woman for it. Thank you, lady Primrose, for housing my thoughts and preserving the feelings that propel these words.

Until next time,
Addie

FOUR
HEBREWS 13:5

My feet have gone to sleep, folded underneath my legs on the cool linoleum floor. I've been completely captivated by the words I've just read. The interesting words of this *Addie*. I feel compelled to find her somehow. The wealth of knowledge she apparently possesses is undoubtedly impressive, but more than that I understand her loneliness, probably better than anyone else could. How she's able to occupy her mind with and even enjoy her work yet is sadly aware of that hollow spot deep within her heart.

Slowly unfolding and rising to my feet like a baby calf standing for the first time, I place the opened diary on the counter and reach for my phone from the dining table.

I know I have the number stored from the last time I had to call and check on the shop's hours. Becky's Bakery, Billie Smith…Yes, here it is.

The phone rings three times before I hear Bobbie's familiar, country twang on the other end.

"Bobbie's Antiques?" she happily answers.

"Hey, Bobbie," I reply, slightly abashed. "It's Blaire Whitfield."

"Well, hey honey! How are you, darlin?" Bobbie asks enthusiastically.

"I'm good! Hope you are…I just wanted to ask you something," I begin.

"I finally got the drawer to open, and I found a diary inside."

"*Really…*" Bobbie makes it sound more like a statement than a question. I can tell she's looking forward to telling the next customer in line all about our conversation.

"I read some of it and found out a little bit about the owner. I wanted to see if you knew anyone named Addie. She's a midwife?" I question with great anticipation. Bobbie knows everyone; surely, she's heard of her.

"No darling, I don't believe that name rings a bell," she lets me down. "That's *interesting* though."

I imagine Bobbie with her readers holding her bangs back, revealing furrowed brows and a deep crevice between them as she leans on the store counter.

"I haven't read very much of it yet because I hate to pry into her personal stuff. I mean, what would I say if I did find her and returned the diary to her? 'Here you can have this back, now that I've read the entire thing?' I don't know, I mean I *really* want to read more because that first entry was so enchanting, but I'm not sure if I should or not," I confess to Bobbie without disclosing any of Addie's business.

"Oh!" I remember. "She has two friends: one named Madge and another named AnnaRuth. Those are sort of unique. Do you know anybody with those names?" I continue to quiz Bobbie.

"No, I don't know *them* either," she replies regretfully. "Can you tell around about when it was written?"

"No hint of any time frame in the first entry, other than it was written in the fall. She talks about it being her favorite time of year," I recall.

"Well, I'm right there with her on that one! I'm about sick of these mosquitoes eating me up every time I try to have a seat on the porch, and this sticky heat has just got to go. I say it every year, but it's just too hot," Bobbie complains in pleasant way.

"Anyway," she continues. "I say the only way you're going to be able to try and locate this woman is to keep on reading. That way, if you do find her you can just explain to her the reason you read her book was to try and figure out who she was so you could get it back to her."

I laugh at this idea. "Bobbie, you could make anything sound innocent!"

"Well, it's true!" she retorts. "Makes perfect sense to me. You don't even have a chance at returning it to her if you don't read on," she assures me.

"You're so funny," I remark.

"You said you thought you picked up the table from a thrift store? Do you remember which one?" I ask, grasping at straws.

"Think it was the little one up here in Weatherford if I'm not mistaken...but I don't really remember, honey," she quickly adds. "It could have been any of them, you know I shop around all over."

My luck. "Well, thank you anyway," I say, trying to hide my disappointment.

"I'm sorry, hon. But if I do hear of any of those names around here, I will be sure and eavesdrop for you!" Bobbie promises. And even as we both giggle, I sense her seriousness.

After ending the call, I'm suddenly tuned in to the shrill whining of Dill by the door.

"Sorry, buddy!" I exclaim, realizing I haven't taken him out since I've been home. I've also apparently been totally ignoring his pleas for who knows how long.

I quickly grab his leash and clip it to his collar as he nearly pulls me down, trying to get outside. I can't help but snicker.

"Gosh! I'm coming, I'm coming!" I promise, though he's only concerned with doing his business and sniffing every blade of grass in the yard.

I let him stay outside for quite a while to make up for my earlier neglect. I wish I could let him run free without his leash, but that's something I plan to allow for him as soon as we move into the country house. Here, we're just too close to the road, and he loves cars far too much to be trusted without a good, thick leash in a strong and vigilant grip.

Once Dill and I have spent a good thirty minutes walking around every inch of the yard twice, we head back inside and each have some iced water before Dill sprawls out across the kitchen floor.

"Dill," I jokingly chide between gulps. "It's a hard life, isn't it?" He doesn't answer.

Placing my glass in the sink, I realize I haven't put away the rest of the things I bought today. I should probably do that, but instead I head to the bedroom where I find my coziest pair of loosely fitting pajamas and change into them, sans brassiere.

I grab my purple heavy fleece blanket from the foot of the bed and drag it down the hall and into the living room where I toss it onto the couch in preparation for a totally nonproductive afternoon.

"Dilly!" I call as I reenter the kitchen to find him still in a prone position on the floor. "Wanna sit with me?" I ask, as I retrieve a box of sugar laden cereal from on top of the refrigerator.

"Come on?" I coax as I walk back into the living room. Dill finally stands and lumbers behind me as I grab the remote control from its place on the fireplace mantle. *The First 48* should be on right now. Getting comfortable on the couch with Dill right next to me, I begin to browse the mystery selections on the TV. As I scan past show after show, my mind drifts back to Addie. She's the real mystery.

"Who am I kidding?" I ask aloud. There's no way I can resist reading more of the diary. And Bobbie is right; there's not much chance of finding Addie if I don't learn more about her. Surely, I will run across something in her writing about a landmark, or *something.*

I quickly toss the blanket off of me and stand from the couch, startling Dill. "Be right back," I promise, before setting off to retrieve Addie's diary from the kitchen counter.

Back on the couch, I nestle underneath the cozy throw with Dill. The sounds of sirens and monotone narration coming from the TV fade until they disappear as I open the cover of the primrose-patterned diary once again.

FIVE
PSALM 139:13-14

I rose early this morning, before the break of dawn. I quickly ground my dark roasted coffee beans by hand before brewing a French press full of steamy robust java. Once steeped, I habitually added a drizzle of honey, a generous glug of Ginger's rich cream from yesterday's milking, and a dash of cinnamon.

After my creamy, revitalizing brew had awakened my senses for the day, I gathered my giant stainless steel milking bucket along with warm washcloths for cleaning Ginger's udder and headed to the barn to call her. She came right in at the sound of my voice, as usual, eager for her morning treat of alfalfa hay with a bit of molasses drizzled on top. She's a bit spoiled, but she deserves it.

I spent about a half hour sitting on my short wooden stool next to Ginger, talking to her as I squeezed her full, leathery teats. I think the best type of therapist is one that grazes fresh grass, looks at you with giant soft brown eyes, and graciously stands while giving you bucket after bucket of frothy, rich goodness.

Like childbirth, sourcing a natural superfood from your own farm animals with your own hands has a certain pure and primal feel that I cannot adequately describe.

Once I'd strained the sweet, creamy liquid through my cheesecloth and had a quick breakfast of fresh eggs and the Garveys' forest-raised pork sausage, I pinned up my unruly mane of hair and prepared for my visit with AnnaRuth. She is forty-two weeks pregnant today.

Upon today's visit, I found her growing increasingly anxious to meet the little one. This is normal and tends to make for a rhythmic labor and smooth delivery as opposed to women who don't feel quite as ready to welcome a baby. I find that the woman's body recognizes any tension, and it prepares for birth only when the mother is calm and ready. However, that never comes for some women, and the baby must come out eventually. So, in those especially nervous or apprehensive mothers, it is extremely important to assist her in working through anything that could be hindering her emotionally, even if counseling happens to take place during the thick of labor.

Luckily, I believe AnnaRuth is not only healthy physically but also spiritually, mentally, and emotionally. She has a strong and loving support system in her doting husband. She has nourished her body well. She has nested. She is armed with knowledge. She is confident and strong. The baby is nestled snugly in the pelvis, headfirst. AnnaRuth will deliver beautifully.

A majority of my patients opt for a surprise gender, mostly because of the possible risks associated with ultrasound technology, but also because it is believed that the excitement of wondering who the new babe will be makes the intensity of labor somewhat lesser. I can remember myself, wondering who Michael was going to be as my body worked him closer and closer into this world. As the rushes came quicker and stronger, I grew more euphoric with anticipation at the realization that I'd soon meet my mysterious, precious, unnamed newborn. And when he came at last, a tsunami of joy and relief overwhelmed me as I reaped my long-awaited reward.

AnnaRuth is among those who have chosen to forgo the ultrasounds with supportive blessings from me.

During our visit, I asked her if she'd like to be checked for cervical dilation, explaining to her that whether or not there was any would not be any indication of when labor would start. I also informed her of the risk of introducing bacteria, thus possible infection. Hearing this, she declined a cervical check, and instead gladly accepted a massage and a warm cup of date-cinnamon bark tea.

I will assume that the most likely reason AnnaRuth's baby isn't quite as ready as its mother is, is because she could have a longer monthly cycle than "normal", therefore the time of conception is off a bit from when she'd believed it to be. This happens often, and while many women do not pay close enough attention to their bodies to know what is happening and when, I highly encourage my clients to begin.

AnnaRuth bounced and rocked gently on her large purple yoga ball as I asked her routine questions and checked her blood pressure. I listened to the baby's heart tones and inconspicuously checked AnnaRuth for any swelling, of which I observed none at all. I stayed and visited her for a nice while, as we enjoyed each other's company. We discussed again, her wishes for the birth.When I left her with a bottle of evening primrose oil and a sachet of raspberry leaf tea, she was much more relaxed and calmly receptive to the coming baby. It cannot be long now.

After I left the expectant mother's charming cottage, I met with my best friend, Madge. We shared a late lunch together in town and caught up on events of each other's current lives. She informed me that she will be spending the next three weeks at her spacious oceanfront beach home. I will keep in touch with her while she is away, and ensure she returns home safely when she promises to. She's sure to return with a handful of soft, colorful sea glass for me, as usual. I own a beautiful collection of the smooth, frosted stones Madge has brought me over the years, mostly shades of blue and green. Once-sharp, shiny bits of glass have been transformed by grazing the velvety sand and tumbling amongst the rhythmic waves.

Like me, Madge has lived alone for many years. Over the years, she has assisted me with many births. Countless times, I've called her to come and help with those special ones where I simply needed an extra hand, or the mother needed more emotional support than I could provide while still tending to pressing physical needs. Madge has grown so comfortable with the physiologic birth process that she would certainly know what to do if she ever needed to deliver a baby alone.

Upon my return home this afternoon, I fed my sourdough master starter a healthy scoop of organic einkorn flour and left it on the counter in its jar to bloom. I will use the bubbly yeast this evening to make a dough for tomorrow morning's breakfast: sourdough ancient grain English muffins. They will be irresistible slathered in golden honey with the homemade butter that Ginger has so generously provided for me.

It is a gray and gloomy day, and dusk is falling fast this evening. So, I think I will go ahead and gather the eggs for the day and settle in. Maybe I'll bake a batch of my "cowboy cookies" to enjoy and share with Madge when she stops by on her way to the beach house tomorrow.

. . . The cookies will have to wait. The eggs can wait as well. AnnaRuth's time has come. I have to go now. I must quickly make a half gallon of switchel for her and then I'm off, to attend my final birth. Here we go...

Addie

SIX
1 TIMOTHY 2:15

Looking up from the words of the mysterious Addie, I try to visualize how she might look. I like to imagine her as a petite lady with long, sleek silver locks pulled back into a neat, granny style nest, wearing a pair of dark rimmed glasses, from which a chain is attached and draping each side of her slender face. I'll bet she wears an apron over long, floral cotton skirts. She probably has warm, well-worn hands, suntanned and calloused, with short, stained nails. The kind that have seen a lot and can do just about anything. I imagine Addie clapping those hard-working hands together in delight as she throws her head back laughing in a joyful moment with a friend. And as I read her words, I read them the way I imagine her voice to sound, as mature as her handwriting and dripping with a wise southern elegance.

Slowly, I take a peek once more at the place where the writing ends and blank pages begin, taking care not to read anything and therefore "spoil the ending." I went to high school with a girl who always read the last line of a book first thing, before she started at the beginning. It made me cringe then, and thinking about it now does too.

It looks like there's as much as I've read, still left to go. I'm hopeful that there will be something in here that will give me a hint of where I can find Addie, but I don't want to devour the journal all in one sitting. Instead, I reach for my phone where I've left it on the coffee table. Jill should be awake by now; she's off tonight.

"Hey. What are you doing?" I ask when she picks up.

"Oh, nothing much. I haven't been up very long, so just stirring around a little. What about you?"

Her voice is gravelly from sleep. I'm probably the first person she's spoken to since waking. Her husband is working day shifts this weekend. I lack an interesting life so much that I even have my best friend's husband's work schedule memorized. How sad.

"Just doing some reading and being lazy. I want to show you something I found. You feel like coming over?"

"Yeah, sure. Just let me put some actual clothes on and brush my hair," she replies. "I'm probably stopping at Starbucks too. You want anything?"

I glance at the empty cereal box next to me on the couch. I probably shouldn't.

"Sure. My usual will be good, thanks."

I'm sure my liver will appreciate me washing down the sugar and preservatives with more sugar and preservatives. I seem to have arrived at a point in my life where I sort of *know* better, but that doesn't necessarily make me *do* any better. And the worst part is that I don't really care too much. Again, sad. But at least I supplement magnesium through my epsom salt baths. Maybe I'll chew a multivitamin tonight.

"Alright, see you in a bit," Jill promises.

"Sounds good. See you soon."

Ending the call, I close Addie's diary and heave myself off the couch.

"You don't have to get up. I'll be back soon," I assure Dill as I cover him with my blanket. Hearing this, he relaxes and lays his head on his fuzzy paws once again.

While waiting for Jill to arrive, I move *Addie's* table to a spot along the kitchen cabinets where Jill won't break her toe on it like Bobbie, when she comes in and I toss my box of cereal crumbs.

I've no sooner tidied up my kitchen clutter and loaded the dishwasher before I hear Jill's Altima pull into the driveway. Dill hears it too, as he perks his ears up and cocks his head sideways.

"It's Jill!" I exclaim. At this, his tail begins thumping the couch cushion like it's a conga underneath the plush throw. He thinks she only comes to visit *him.*

"Knock, knock!" I hear her call from the garage entry.

"Come in," I respond, although she's already in and standing in the kitchen holding a drink tray full of sugary caffeine. Among our cappuccinos I see a tiny cup full of whipped cream, for none other than Dill, I have no doubt.

Jill sets the tray of coffees on the counter and goes for Dill's treat first.

"Diiiiiillll!" She calls, in three syllables.

"Look what I've got!" She peeks around the kitchen wall at Dill laying on the couch, as she leans forward with the tiny cup of sweet fluffy cream in her outstretched hand. At this, he immediately hops off the couch and bolts toward Jill, his tail like a windshield wiper during a rain deluge.

He licks up the treat in about two swipes of his drooly tongue and then continues to try and lick a hole straight through the cup, as Jill holds it out for him.

"Dill? Do you have manners?" He ignores me as I reach for my own treat from the kitchen counter.

Once Dill is satisfied and has ambled over to his water dish, Jill joins me on the couch with her fancy coffee.

"What's up?" She asks, pulling her knees up to her chest with her free hand, careful not to slosh sticky coffee onto the couch.

I pick the diary up from where I left it on the arm of the couch and hold it up.

"This," I reply as if that'll be the only explanation she needs.

"What's that?"

"A diary I found. Did you see that little white table there in the kitchen?" I ask.

"I didn't," Jill admits. "I was too busy spoiling your dog."

"Well," I begin, placing my cup on the coffee table. "I bought a beautiful old nightstand at Bobbie's today. For nothing, basically. Drawer was stuck but I finally got it open and when I did, I found *this.*" I hold the floral notebook up again, wearing an excited grin like I've just won something remarkable. And I did, in my opinion.

"I read some, and then decided I needed to find this woman so the first thing I did was call Bobbie to see if she could help. She couldn't, but I'm not giving up that easily. I really want to know her," I confess.

"Why is that?" Jill asks with anticipation. She unfolds her knees and slides closer to me on the brown suede sofa looking longingly at the diary in my hand.

As I recount what I know of Addie's life so far and read aloud some of the unique chronicles she's recorded, Jill seems to hang onto every word, listening intently. She's just as intrigued as I am with the beautiful words written by my wise new friend who doesn't even know I exist. But, maybe she will.

When I finish, stopping where Addie has just apparently gotten an important call from AnnaRuth, an enthralled Jill smiles widely at the thought of the imaginary author.

"Wow," she comments as she slowly shakes her head and sips from her disposable coffee cup. "She seems like a really neat lady!"

"Isn't it *great?*" I exclaim.

"I think you can definitely find her if you keep asking around," Jill replies optimistically.

"I know. I think so too," I agree. "Do you think I'm wrong for reading this?" I ask.

"I mean, am I violating Addie's privacy? I can't help but think if I *do* find her then I'll be ashamed to admit to her that I read her personal thoughts."

"Oh, no. I don't think so," Jill assures me. "And I think you have the greatest chance of finding her and returning her diary if you *do* read more of it."

"*Thank* you! Bobbie and I thought the exact same thing. But it still feels a little intrusive or something. I don't know. I mean, don't get me wrong. I'm still going to read the rest. How could I not? But I needed the reassurance that I'm not doing something totally wrong," I shrug as I bring my coffee cup to my lips.

"Oh, I think you're fine," Jill says with the wave of her hand as she settles into the couch. "What are you going to do otherwise, throw it away? That wouldn't do a bit of good."

"That's a good point you have there," I state with satisfaction.

"Mmhmm. I wonder if we should be drinking raw cows' milk instead of almond milk," Jill ponders aloud as she gives her coffee a look of skepticism.

"I kinda wondered about that too," I admit with a light snicker.

"She seems like she's got it all figured out while enjoying the best of health to boot. Too bad I can't just call her up and pick her brain on these things. I'm definitely excited to read more into the sage mind of Addie the midwife, though." I raise an impish brow and turn the corner of my mouth into a sly half-smile.

"I don't want to read it all at once though, you know what I mean? I want to *savor* it," I explain, as I tug on an invisible necklace with my right fist, adding valid but unnecessary drama.

Jill giggles. "I know what you mean," she assures me with her classic genuine smile as she tousles her shiny, black ponytail.

Then solemnly, I continue. "I think my daddy would have liked her. Grandmama, too." I dwell on the memories of the two of them for a moment until Jill interrupts my thoughts.

"Yeah, I bet they would have," she says, sincere sympathy in her eyes.

"Well," I stand from the couch and change the subject.

"What are you doing for supper? You want to grab some take-out?" I ask, my mind immediately flashing to Addie in her kitchen as I have it pictured. I wonder what she'd say about the habits I've implemented for myself. I imagine she'd make me a farm-fresh meal with a side of buttered sourdough bread and some sort of herbal tea. My heart starts to melt and drip warmth into my stomach at that brief but satisfying thought.

"Sure. I'll grab something for Todd, too. He'll be home in an hour," Jill agrees as she glances at the clock on the fireplace mantle.

"We'd better be going, then. Let me just put on some clothes right quick." I would actually rather eat dirt than put on jeans. "Well, at least a bra," I add. "You pick and I'll order!" I call as I head down the hallway to the bedroom.

SEVEN
HOSEA 14:4

The repetitive duck quacking sound coming from the phone next to my pillow reminds me that my leisurely day off is behind me. Back to the grind I'll go, as soon as I muster the will to heave myself from the warm bed. The old folks need their pills. With one sleepy eye half open, I glance at my noisy and incredibly bright phone and hit the snooze button. Dill is already whining and pawing at the mattress, as he does every time my alarm goes off. How dare anything disturb his precious sleep?

Sitting up in bed, I rub my burning, gritty eyes and look sleepily over at Dill. "Hush, you've got it made," I tell him. "I have to go to work to provide your Milk Bones and kibble." He's already snoring again.

I head to the bathroom and warm a washcloth to wipe my face with before dressing in my solid black scrubs which will have to be lint rolled. It doesn't take very long for me to get ready for work. A clean face and hair pulled up into a messy bun is usually as good as it gets. After all, I'm going to be returning home tonight wearing someone else's bodily fluids, so I don't see much point in trying to look too glamorous. Plus, I'm the kind of girl that would rather spend that extra ten minutes sleeping.

Dill will get a few more minutes of sleep himself while I pack my lunchbox, before I coax him out of bed and take him out to do his business. I realize I should have probably gone grocery shopping yesterday as I scan the refrigerator for some lunch. It's pretty slim pickings, but chances are I won't even have time to eat it anyway. I finally settle on a pack of beef jerky, a tangerine, and a cheese stick. More than likely, I'll be pulling pieces of jerky from my pocket in between patient rooms during the afternoon medication pass.

After starting my cup of coffee brewing and grabbing a Pop Tart for the road, I call for Dill. But as usual, I have to go tug on and aggravate him until he reluctantly jumps down off the bed and shakes his ears in protest. I know he'll be less cranky when it comes time for his morning treat, though.

The drive to work is pleasantly stimulating. I've chosen my *Good Vibes Only* coffee tumbler for my sugary medium roast brew, dropped a little extra of my *"invigorating"* blend of essential oils onto my travel oil diffuser, and I've spent the entire drive engaged in thoughts of Addie.

Aside from trying to think of ways I can track her down in a non-stalkerish way, I'm feeling inspired by her apparent wisdom, the simple way in which she lives in contentment, and most of all, how she's been able to overcome grief and live a fulfilling life despite great loss. I feel the spark of hope that I might someday be on the other side of despair, too. Maybe there will come a day when I am able to live a joy-filled life, free from the daily sting of loneliness.

I realize, as I turn into the parking lot of Sunny Meadows, I've been lost in thought for the entire drive to work. The golden morning sun is just starting to peek over the roof of the tall familiar brick building as I habitually speed to my favorite parking spot. It's my favorite for no particular reason at all, but it puts me in a bad mood when someone else is parked in it.

Inside, the faint odor of talcum powder and urine in the cool sterile air is too familiar to be offensive. I bound through the nurses' station and around the corner to the time clock, my tennis shoes squeaking on the freshly buffed tiles. I quickly enter my employee ID number before spinning around on my heel with another squeak and heading back into the warm, carpeted nurses' station.

"Well, good morning," I hear a familiar voice greet me as I enter the little room. It's Sharon, sitting at the desk apparently finishing up her notes. Though not nearly as thorough as Jill, I don't mind following her shift too much. At least I know the patients have been medicated according to doctors' orders, and I'm not likely to find anyone lying on the floor, telling me they'd fallen out of bed hours before.

"Morning!" I chime as I approach the wobbly wooden table where I'll sit to receive her report. Carefully placing my work bag and lunchbox on the table, I take a seat and begin digging through my bag in search of my name badge and things I'll fill my scrub pockets with: ink pens, scissors, hand sanitizer. They'll hold a wider assortment of things by the end of the day.

"Well, aren't you chipper this morning," Sharon comments as she peers up at me from her paperwork, eyebrows elevated. "Did you have an extra cup of coffee?"

I feel a touch of ridicule in the assumed rhetorical question, but I'm unbothered by it. Truthfully, everyone is probably used to me dragging in, still half asleep and barely on time for my shift. It usually takes me a good hour on the job to gain any momentum. Of course, there are some days where I walk into a whirlwind of chaos and have no choice but to hit the floor running. That doesn't appear to be the case this morning, thank Heavens.

A half-hearted snicker escapes my throat. "I don't know, I'm just in a good mood today. I guess I slept really well."

"How was it last night?" I ask as I test out my pen on a scrap of paper.

"It was a pretty good night," Sharon answers, as if she's pleasantly surprised.

I'm oddly optimistic about the workday and its possible sequence of events. Ordinarily, I'd take down the report of all my patients and automatically assume that catastrophe would soon strike my assigned hall because in my mind, if it's going to happen, it's going to happen on Blaire's watch.

Today feels different. I'm hopeful that the day will run smoothly while realizing the possibility that it may not. Either way, I'm mentally prepared for whatever I, or those in my care, might encounter.

The report Sharon gave me was pretty bland, but that's a good thing in this setting. There is a new patient that was admitted yesterday who has a wound vac on her left thigh and is receiving IV antibiotics. I'm glad I didn't have to do that admission assessment and paperwork; however, a part of me hopes that the wound vac sounds its alarm today to let me know that it isn't suctioning properly, because completely redressing and connecting those things are among my favorite things to do.

Although Sharon assured me that all of my patients are alive and well and without complaints, I walk the hall and personally peek my head into each room for myself. Some of the patients are still sleeping peacefully; others are getting ready for the day with the help of a very valuable aide. Assigned to my hall today is Meg, thank God. She's the best aide in all of Sunny Meadows, in my opinion. I feel at such ease when I know she's on the front lines, tending to the basic needs of the patients and calling for my assistance whenever appropriate. She's also a lot of fun and helps keep my moods lighter on those especially tough days.

After making my round checking on the patients of the 100-wing, I stop by the snack room to stock my medicine cart with applesauce and orange juice in preparation for the morning medication round. These additions will help wash down the cupful of pills that each patient takes.

As I exit the closet of a room with my arms full of large plastic carafes and cold tubs of puréed fruits, I see the 200-wing nurse, Lisa, rounding the corner of the nurses' station carrying her lunch bag. Suddenly, I realize I'm twenty minutes early for my shift. That explains why Sharon was still charting on all the patients who reportedly did nothing but sleep all night. Maybe that also explains some of the passive sarcasm I caught. I have no clue how I managed this; I'm never early. However, learning this gives me an extra spark of energy as I walk quickly to my medicine cart to get started doling out the dope. Maybe I'll finish the breakfast round before lunchtime.

I push the monstrous cart the short distance to the first room on 100-wing and park it there, stopping to flip the switch for the hall lights. The night shift nurses always darken as much of the place as possible. I think they must make their rounds checking on patients with an oil lamp, like Florence Nightingale herself.

I can hear their chatter in the nurses' station as Sharon recounts last night to Lisa, who is assigned to the 200-wing. Another nurse, Brittany, will take charge of 300-wing. Glancing at my watch, I note that it's seven o' clock sharp. Brittany should be clocking in any second.

As I unlock the medicine cart with a noisy clatter that's unavoidable, I immediately hear the voice of Miss Cathy in the room I'm parked just outside. Miss Cathy is awake and waiting for her morning pills, all eighteen of them. And she wants to make sure she's first.

"Blaaaaaaa-ire?" Miss Cathy calls from her recliner where she chooses to sleep. Apparently, she can't breathe well while in her bed, even with the head fully elevated.

"Yes ma'am?" I lean into her doorway to face her.

"I need a pain pill," she requests with a smile, while stretching both arms.

"Okay. What's your pain level?" I ask, already knowing the answer.

"Nine and a half," she sings.

"Alright, and where is the pain, Miss Cathy?" I ask, stepping into her room and appearing genuinely concerned. It's probably her back, if I had to guess. She might change it up this morning, though.

"My…neck," she sings again.

"Uh, oh. Did you sleep in a bad position?" I ask.

"Yes! I can't get comfortable in this old thing!" She slaps both hands down on the arms of the giant brown recliner that's stained with grape jelly and orange Cheeto dust.

"Okay, I'll get you something. Would you want to try some Biofreeze first and see if that helps instead?" I offer, knowing it's going to be a 'heck no' from Miss Cathy.

"No!" She adamantly casts down that notion with an exaggerated frown. "That stuff doesn't work. I need a pain pill. Two if I can get them."

"Alright, I'll see what I can do," I agree.

Among Miss Cathy's colorful array of various medications she takes every morning, she receives Abilify for her depression, which causes her to have involuntary tremors called tardive dyskinesia, for which she takes Primidone, which causes dizziness, for which she takes Antivert, which causes dry mouth, for which she will request a cup of Biotene. And so on, and so on. Times eighteen, plus any additional medication she requests, that she has a standing order for.

I document her pre-medication pain level and then pop a Percocet out of the bubble pack. I will need to order a refill for these today; she only has six left which will last twenty-four hours, at best. I scribble this onto my to-do list and continue to fill the small cup with Miss Cathy's morning pills.

As I pull medication after medication from the large drawer, I can't help but wonder what Addie would say about all of this. The medications and their side effects, the drug interactions that will happen inside Miss Cathy's poorly functioning body, the toxic load her organs constantly bear.

I have always been aware of the detriment that is caused, literally by my hands, as I spoon feed dozens of powdered pills in applesauce or pudding to patients like Miss Cathy, but the fact seems significantly more profound when compared to Addie's apparent lifestyle. I imagine she's made mindful choices in a worthwhile attempt to prevent the kind of diseases that riddle a majority of my patients. And I imagine Miss Cathy is among those who have never given much thought at all to the consequences of their daily habits. Realizing this, I feel a knot form in the depths of my stomach as I quickly develop a fear for my future health. Iced sugar pastries for breakfast? Come on, Blaire. You can do better.

In addition to my crappy diet, exercising my rights as an American citizen is the extent of that verb in my life. I feel I could benefit from the counsel of Addie. Except, I have no idea where to begin to look for her. Honestly, that old table could have come from anyplace in the southern US. Or beyond, even.

Today though, for the first time in ages, I'm not letting pessimism rule my thought life. Someday, I'll find her. I have to find the woman who gave me a pinch of hope amidst the melancholy monotony I've grown so comfortable with.

After preparing all of Miss Cathy's ordered medications, requested pain pill included, I add a

Compazine tablet for nausea to a separate medicine cup and set it aside. She will need it in approximately fifteen minutes; however, she absolutely will not accept it with the rest of her medicines. She will wait until I'm next door, carefully pushing Mr. Carter's medications through his feeding tube before she begins shouting for a nausea pill and making voluntary gagging sounds. I cap a lid on the small medicine cup containing the Compazine before stashing it in my shirt pocket in preparation for this impending outburst.

As I sign out each of the twenty medications I've cupped up for Miss Cathy, I can see with my peripheral vision that someone is approaching my right. It's probably Mr. Baldwin. He comes every morning without fail, to feed his wife her breakfast and sit with her for a few hours. First, though, he comes to find me to ask how Mrs. Baldwin slept. I simply cannot imagine how nice it must feel to have someone be so devoted to you.

Sitting the water pitcher back in its spot on the medicine cart, I look to my right, ready to greet Mr. Baldwin with his newspaper and quad cane in hand. I immediately feel my smile loosen ever so slightly as I realize it's not Mr. Baldwin approaching me. I guess I'd never even considered it a possibility of being anyone else at this hour.

But, lo and behold. It's a police officer. I wonder if one of the patients has called 9-1-1. It sure wouldn't be the first time.

"Mornin' ma'am," he greets me with friendliness in his tone and a subtle nod of his head, like a true southern gentleman.

I wonder if it's evident in my body language that I've been slightly taken aback as he approaches my cart. "Morning," I reply. "Can I help you?"

"I'm looking for a patient named Mrs. Margaret Simms." He awaits my reply from an arm's length away, shifting his weight to his right hip.

There's no patient here by that name. She's not on my hall, and I also know for a fact that she isn't a patient on any of the other two halls either, because I've been asked to help with all of the recent admissions.

"Hmm," I pretend to ponder this as I nibble at my bottom lip.

"I'm afraid you'll have to contact the family about *that* patient." I wince my regrets to him.

He leans toward me a bit, eyes wide with apparent concern. "Why?" He whispers. "She didn't pass away, did she?" He seems legitimately worried.

Basically, I'm prohibited from telling anyone anything about any patient who may or may not even be an actual patient. I get that, sort of. If I were a patient, I'd want my privacy protected too. However, I'm not a patient and neither is Margaret Simms. At least, not here at Sunny Meadows.

I stifle a giggle. "Well, I'm not at liberty to say — um… Are you sure you're at the right facility?" It's the best I can come up with. Hopefully he isn't an idiot.

He snickers. "You've never heard of her." He states as a realization rather than a question. Good, he's not an idiot.

"Afraid not." Technically I haven't broken any laws.

"Well, shoot," he says, seemingly a bit embarrassed. "I've come to the wrong place, I guess."

"Have you tried Aspen Acres over on Sugar Ridge Road?" I ask. "It's the nearest nursing facility to this one, and people come here looking for its patients often, and vice versa."

"Yeah, maybe *that's* the one," he admits. "Mrs. Margaret is an elder at my church and she's just had some sort of heart surgery. She was supposed to be released from the hospital yesterday. I could have sworn they said she would be coming *here* for rehab, but I guess I heard wrong."

"Well, I hope you find her, Officer...." I intentionally squint at his badge... "Baker." I read aloud from the shiny rectangular badge pinned to his left chest.

"It's Joseph." He corrects me with a wink as he very quickly steals a glance at my left hand.

My goodness. Is this man flirting with me?

Then, as if answering my silent question, he continues. "You know, I sure am glad I messed up. I might've missed out on seeing the prettiest nurse there ever was." He smiles broadly, revealing perfectly aligned, pearly white teeth.

I feel my face flush. "Oh, whatever!" I declare dramatically with a nervous laugh before looking down at the small cupful of pills in my hand.

"It's okay to accept a compliment, you know?" He chuckles, apparently aware of my sudden embarrassment, which leads to increased embarrassment.

"Oh, I know. And thank you. I guess it's just not every day I receive that kind of compliment," I admit.

"Usually, the best I get is like 'that didn't hurt at all' or something." I laugh but it's true.

"I can't believe *that,*" he comments with a look of skepticism.

"Believe it, Joe," I retort, before pursing my lips in an attempt at total seriousness.

"Oh, it's Joe already, huh?" He snickers.

At this, my face cracks into a smile. "I'm sorry. Do you hate it when people call you Joe?"

"Well, normally yes…I guess it's okay, though" he says with a soft smile as he slightly cocks his head to the side, as if carefully considering something.

"Well," he continues. "It was nice meeting you— " Now it's his turn to hone in on my badge. "…Blaire," he reads aloud. "I guess I'll let you get back to work. I hate that I bothered you."

"Oh, no. No bother," I assure him. "Sorry you didn't find who you were looking for."

With that, he fixes his chestnut-colored eyes on mine and holds them there for several grounding seconds before winking once more.

"Thank you anyway, Blaire," he says with a brief wave of his hand as he turns and heads back down the long green-and-white tiled hallway, toward the exit door.

As I watch him walk away, the jingle of his keys fades and is slowly but surely replaced by the monotonous buzzing of call bells and the morning news blaring from patients' televisions.

"Wow!" I nearly jump out of my skin at the familiar voice of Meg's exclamation.

"Meg!" I chide, clutching at my pounding chest. "What are you doing?" I know what she's doing. She's lurking around the corner being nosey.

"I was helping Mr. Harris to tie his shoes when we heard an unfamiliar voice out here sounding super — ahem…friendly, so we peeked out to see what was going on. And you two didn't even notice us in the doorway. You were too busy gazing into each other's eyes," she grins and bats her own mascara lacquered lashes.

"Oh, please!" I beg dramatically with the wave of my hand.

"I think I heard Mrs. Hagan calling for you," I fib. Meg and I both know it's time for her to buzz for her coffee any second, though.

"Yeah, she's not calling me," she states matter-of-factly as she leans over onto my medicine cart and props herself on both elbows.

"You *know*…if you can stay ahead of the needs, your day will go much smoother," I remind her with a sneer. We both try to help each other to follow this motto whenever we work together, and I feel very much like holding her accountable right now. Of course, the strategy doesn't always work for me. In fact, most days I can't keep up with all the needs, much less remain ahead of them. But it's not due to a lack of trying.

"Yeah, yeah," Meg sighs as she withdraws from her resting place and slinks away down the corridor, headed toward Mrs. Hagan's room. "He was really c-u-u-u-u-te," she sings, glancing over her shoulder as she anticipates my reaction. "Just saying," she quickly adds with a shrug as she enters the room, the light above the door now aglow.

Suddenly the smirky grin falls from my face as I look down at the cup of pills I'm still holding and remember Miss Cathy. My heart drops into my stomach as I realize that she should be shooting fireworks off into the hallway by now. I frantically lock the medicine cart and prepare to jet into her room to check on her when I hear a familiar sound intertwined with the others that are raining all around me.

My heart rate decelerates as I exhale with relief at the realization that the sound I've been tuning out is Miss Cathy attempting to inhale the drapes in her sleep. Miss Cathy, whose pain level is nine and a half. Steadying my vehement haste and rapid respirations, I gather all of her pills, inhalers, eye drops, and insulin shots and head into her room again to wake her for the awe-inspiring medication administration.

Once Miss Cathy and the rest of the patients on my assigned wing have all been medicated according to doctors' orders, I and my colossal medicine cart slowly make our way back up the long hallway and park it outside the nurses station. That was actually a pleasant morning round. Nobody spit their medications in my face, pulled an IV line out, or required the Heimlich maneuver.

As I carry the unused portions of pudding and applesauce back to the refrigerator, I spot Brittany near the end of the long hallway, still hard at work delivering the morning medications to her patients on the 300-wing. I send her a quick but friendly wave before dipping into the nourishment room.

I've been happily aware of the pleasant course my morning has taken, from Addie in my ear, quietly guiding my thoughts and attitude, to being flirted with by an attractive cop. It suddenly occurs to me that beyond this strangely blissful morning I'm experiencing, there's also the exciting portion of my life that hasn't crossed my mind at all this morning.

The farmhouse, of course. Like receiving a package from the mailman that you'd forgotten you ordered, I realize I actually haven't thought of the house once finding Addie's diary. This is shocking, considering how much I longingly fantasized about it before. I guess it sort of shifts the perspective when you compare the two dramas that both recently found themselves a vibrant part of my life.

Though I'm eager to read more into Addie's life, I find that I'm content with routinely performing my duties with the secret satisfaction of anticipating the next chapter tucked away in the depths of my mind. I smile at the realization that I actually have things to look forward to, for the first time in my adult life.

I silently make plans to both read a chapter from Addie's diary tonight and make a phone call first thing Monday morning to see how the pest inspection on the farmhouse went. It should have been done yesterday, and prior to finding the diary, I would have definitely already called to check for any possible update on the process.

I glance down the hall perpendicular, where Lisa is still hard at work on the 200-wing.

Our facility hasn't joined the rest of the world in electronic charting, so I will head into the nurses' station where I'll document on twelve Medicare patients and six others who have acute issues, with hand-written notes. I actually don't mind so much. Although my right hand and my penmanship will both be suffering by the time I finish, I take pride in writing very thorough nurse's notes. You never know when one of those notes might wind up in the middle of a court case or something.

Just as I sit down to begin charting on the first patient, which happens to be Miss Cathy, I hear a familiar voice coming from the speaker on the telephone that hangs on the wall. It's Cindy, the receptionist, buzzing already this morning.

"Hello? Anybody down there?" she hollers.

"Good morning," I answer.

"The hospital is on line one, calling report for 100-hall," Cindy shouts through the speaker. She must not realize I'm standing right in front of the phone.

"Report?" I ask, shocked. I didn't know I was getting a new admission today.

"That's what she said. I just work here," Cindy answers with a bland tone.

"Okay, I'll pick up. Thanks—" But she's already hung up.

"Well then," I say to myself as I reach for the phone.

I take the receiver down from its base and punch the flashing red "Line 1" button as I sit down and grab a scrap of paper from the desk drawer.

"This is Blaire, how can I help you?" I answer in my most professional "phone voice".

"Hi, Blaire. This is Gina from over at the hospital." Gina sounds as pleased to be alive as Cindy did. I think Eeyore must be her spirit animal.

"I'm needing to give a report to the nurse for room one-oh-three," she slowly spills out in a thick southern drawl. I don't think Gina learned about the phone voice thing when she was in training *over at the hospital.*

"That's me," I reply as I reach into my shirt pocket and retrieve my pen. "You can go ahead with the report."

"Okay…" she begins as she clicks away on a keyboard in the background.

"You said your name's Blaire, right?"

"Yep!" I answer.

"Okay," Gina says again. "So, I'm calling a report from West Surgical…She was supposed to be discharged yesterday, but she kept de-satting so the cardiologist wanted to keep her one more night…"She draws each word out long and slow.

"She's held her own all day for me, though. She's been at ninety-eight percent on two liters of oxygen…" Gina continues, as I begin to take notes.

"Seventy-three year old female… She had a C.A.B.G. done on Thursday. Tolerated well." I hear the rustling of papers as she continues to pour the words into my ear as slowly as if they were chilled molasses.

"She has a six-inch incision to her mid-sternum. Chest tube was removed this morning. Dressings are dry and intact. She is alert and oriented to her surroundings — well, shoot… you would probably like to know her name, wouldn't you?" Her voice is still yet to indicate the hint of a smile on her face.

At last, she continues to speak as she provides me with the name of my soon-to-be new patient.

"This is… Mrs. Margaret Simms…" her voice trails off as I drop my pen and nearly drop the phone as well.

I regain awareness that I'm still on the phone with Gina as her voice suddenly becomes audible again, as if I've been submerged in water. I glance down at my scrap of paper to see that I've scribbled Margaret Simms' last set of vital signs, her ambulatory status, and even the last time she visited the toilet. I don't even remember hearing or writing any of it, but if I missed anything I will find out when I assess Mrs. Simms myself.

Once Gina has finished giving me the run-down and lets me know that EMS is scheduled to transport Mrs. Simms over this afternoon, I hang the phone receiver back onto its base, kicking the long curly cord out of the way, and quickly steal another peek down each hallway. I don't see any sign of Meg. She must be in a patient's room. I think I'll keep this new information to myself for now; Meg will find out soon enough.

I make quick but thorough notes in each patient's chart in an attempt to stay ahead of any obstacle that may prevent me from a smooth-sailing workday. Gina said that EMS would transport Mrs. Simms over between two and three o' clock, but I am aware that she may not arrive until at least six-thirty. Either way, I do my best to prepare for the admission process that I'll be completing whenever she does arrive.

I start filling out the paperwork that I can get a headstart on, though most of it will have to be done after I assess and interview Mrs. Simms. Once I scribble down as much as possible before the new patient's arrival, I place the packet of documents in a folder and take them with me to my medicine cart. I don't want them to get misplaced while I'm checking my diabetic patients' blood sugar levels.

Rounding the corner of the dimly lit nurses' station and heading toward my cart, I nearly get run over by Brittany who is quickly approaching with her medicine cart.

"Whoa, sorry!" Brittany shrieks with wide eyes as she tries to stop the cart from smashing into me. Luckily, I saw her coming and had a chance to escape her path at the last moment.

I laugh as I scurry to safety against the wall, clutching my paperwork tightly against my chest.

"You're getting an admission?" Brittany asks, nodding at the folder.

"Yep, coming to 103 this afternoon," I reply.

"Oh man, a weekend admission. That's a bummer."

"Let me know if you need any help," Brittany offers.

"Thank you," I reply, as I wave the folder full of documents. "I should be fine, though. This patient *seems* like a piece of cake, according to the nurse that gave me the report. You know how that goes, though." I stifle a laugh.

"I *do* know how that goes, unfortunately. Well, let me know if you need any help once the patient gets here and you see for yourself how she is, then."

"Will do," I promise as I step over to the medicine cart and prepare to make the noon round checking blood glucose levels and administering insulin shots and stomach pills.

EIGHT
PSALM 23

Despite the surprise admission, the workday continued to flow smoothly. Mrs. Simms did indeed turn out to be as low maintenance as Gina had told me she would be. She's as sweet as cake, and as the icing on that cake, she only takes very few medications. The pharmacy representative will drop those off tonight after I'm long gone.

Once I gave Sharon the report of each patient this evening, I clocked out and left feeling tired but still oddly anticipatory of something joyous. Instead of the monotonous routine that I'm so accustomed to, as I pulled into my driveway tonight, I experienced an emotional foretaste of what my life could possibly look like this time next year. Or, this time next month, even.

Up until two days ago, I'd only ever thought about what I was doing at a particular moment, never really looking forward to anything ahead. After driving home from work, I'd habitually slink to the door and shove my key into the deadbolt while thinking negative thoughts about my humble home that has served me well, however unappreciated it has been. I suddenly feel a twinge of guilt as I realize that I'll soon be leaving this house that I never truly loved. I find myself hoping that someone will replace me who will take care of every inch of the house, instead of just taking shelter within it. I hope a family with children moves in and leaves their mark on every door jamb and threshold, piling shoes by the door and toys across the floor.

I have occasionally hung baskets of brightly colored petunias and geraniums around the front porch, and I've kept the lawn manicured to my taste. That's pretty much the extent of how I've bothered to make this house resemble a home, or to accentuate its humble and quirky characteristics.

Dill was very excited to greet me tonight, as usual. He doesn't care where we live, as long as I'll scratch his ears, share my bed, and feed him. He isn't going to know what to think about being able to roam for acres at the new place.

As I'm undressing for the hot bathtub awaiting me in the next room, I hear my phone *ding* alerting me of a text message. Dill, who is laying across the bed, cocks his head to one side at the sound of my phone. I could receive a thousand *dings* a day and he'd do it every time. It's really adorable.

I reach into my opened work bag at the foot of the bed and grab my glowing phone.

New Text Message from
Aaron Bailey, Real Estate Agent:
Hi, Blaire. Sorry it's late. Got a closing date on the house. Friday at 10 o 'clock. Everything is

good to go with termite inspection. Previous owners took care of the land surveying costs. Things are moving along quickly! Talk soon. - Aaron

A shriek of uncontainable bliss escapes me. This time, Dill barks.

"We're moving, boy!" I exclaim. He paws the bed, mirroring my excitement.

I lay my phone on the vanity and happily dance across the carpet to the adjoined bathroom. I'm promptly followed by Dill who collapses onto his spot on the bathroom rug where he'll wait for me to finish my nightly bath.

Then suddenly, as if her name was written on the bathroom mirror in front of me, I remember Addie. Somehow, I'd temporarily dismissed my plans to retrieve her diary as soon as possible upon returning home. I glance at the clock above the oak dresser to find that it's only ten minutes past eight. I have plenty of time to read the next chapter before Dill and I retire to bed, but truthfully, I would make time regardless of what the clock said.

After skipping over to the nightstand to grab the floral notebook, I race back to turn the water off before the tub overflows.

"I'm back. See, I didn't go far," I have to assure Dill as he hesitantly takes his place on the bathroom rug once more.

The warm oasis consumes my body from the neck down as I sink into the salty retreat and begin to read Addie's intriguing scrawl in its thin black ink.

NINE
JOHN 16:21

*A*nnaRuth's baby was born two weeks ago, today. She had called me at 3:15 on the humid Thursday afternoon and said that she was having fairly intense surges along with a bit of bloody show in her panties. The pains were coming at five-minute intervals and lasting around a minute each, she told me over the phone in a voice that cracked with raw emotion. I told her I'd be over right away and urged her to rest as much as possible and to take long, deep breaths. Then, I hastily and excitedly gathered some things and changed into a well-worn cotton jumper with lots of large pockets before heading out to the soon-to-be new mother's house.

It's a fifteen-minute drive from my farm in the country to AnnaRuth's home on the outskirts of town. I arrived at the small quaint cottage at a quarter till four and found AnnaRuth pacing over the creaky hardwood floors of her bedroom, rubbing her large bare belly as the surges of pain came one after the other; strong, rhythmic waves peaking and then slowly falling to rest *until the next crashing wave came, surely but steadily. She was uncomfortable lying or sitting; walking seemed to be of the most comfort to her. The vintage, blue-bladed oscillating fan turned slowly and followed her as she paced back and forth in time to her long, shaky breaths.*

I checked AnnaRuth's blood pressure and then I listened to the baby's heartbeat with the fetoscope. It sounded nothing short of wonderful, although I could tell that the baby wasn't in the most perfect position to descend smoothly into the birth canal.

Without sharing that information with AnnaRuth right away, I continued to monitor her progress. She paced around the perimeter of her tidy cottage home, taking sips of the grapefruit-lemon switchel that I made for her. I asked if her pain was very intense in her lower back, and she said that it was indeed. I took that opportunity to suggest some changes in her body's stance that I felt would aid in moving the baby into optimal birthing position. AnnaRuth gladly accepted my advice and posed just as I instructed her to, groaning low and deep, from the depths of her intuitive core.

I stayed close by, monitoring AnnaRuth quietly from a dim corner of the softly lit bedroom so as not to crowd or cause her any stress. The smell of sweet jasmine and clary sage filled the quaint cottage that would soon be a sacred birth space. I slipped away to the kitchen to retrieve things as I needed them...a bowl of iced water with rags to cool the laboring mother from the heat of childbirth; a fresh jar of coconut oil which would serve as a gentle lubricant.

Earlier in the afternoon, I quickly located a quart-sized jar from the kitchen cupboard and used it to make a strong, fragrant herbal tea from lavender, calendula, rosemary, and lemon balm – all purposely grown in my plentiful summer tea garden. Once cooled a bit, I placed the medicinal infusion in the refrigerator and let AnnaRuth's husband, Samuel know that the tea was for AnnaRuth's bottom in a day or two. "...So, don't drink it," I advised him with a wink. AnnaRuth was able to find humor in that and managed a brief laugh between the ever-increasing spasms that would soon become powerful enough to push forth the precious new baby from within her womb. I offered her a tablespoon full of lavender-infused honey that I'd steeped together in the weeks prior.

She accepted and enjoyed the honey, which served as a source of energy but also provided a sense of calmness. Then, without disturbing her things, I softly sifted through AnnaRuth's basket of baby linens she'd prepared at her bedside and took out a soft receiving blanket with little gray sheep printed on it.

At 5 o' clock pm, when the labor pains were like electrical volts surging through her midsection and AnnaRuth was no longer getting much of a break from them, I heard the familiar sound of water hitting the floor with a forceful slap, and immediately following was an involuntary grunt forced up through AnnaRuth's throat as the baby slipped quietly downward and prepared to exit its mother's body.

At the sound of imminent new life, I swiftly and discreetly took my place at AnnaRuth's bottom while Samuel remained in his place by her side. With my bum knee complaining most obnoxiously, I dug a pair of clean rubber gloves from within my deep jumper pocket and dipped out a dollop of coconut oil from the jar.

AnnaRuth felt most comfortable giving birth in a squatted position as her hands clung tightly to the cherrywood bedpost adorned with intricate carvings of rice stalks. Sweat beaded across her chest and down her back as adrenaline pulsed through her powerful body making her opened thighs tremble.

As the baby's head began bulging from AnnaRuth, I offered very little intervention but greased the mother's tight skin around the baby's deep purple head. I gave no commands, but instead whispered how wonderfully she was delivering, and that she would be holding her baby very soon.

Over the years, I've found that in most cases laboring mothers greatly appreciate the hands-off approach that I implement whenever possible, and in all cases, the mother instinctively knows what to do without being obnoxiously instructed.

Low, gravelly groans escaped AnnaRuth's lips as she breathed her baby downward, its perfect little face emerging from the elastic skin around it. A little folded hand was up by the face - a nuchal hand. I applied some pressure to AnnaRuth's tight, bulging bottom but despite that, I saw the skin begin to tear away from the baby's head as bright red blood began to flow from the jagged wound and drip onto the hardwood floor. An impatient, vigorous pusher she was. But I didn't blame her.

"You're doing great, Mama!" I distinctly remember exclaiming through salty, silent tears as I sat beneath AnnaRuth's bottom and continued to support it while Samuel held tightly to her upper body and softly whispered intimate words of admiration.

With one final surge from within, the rest of the baby's slippery, blue body fell into my hands. I quickly grabbed the cotton sheep-adorned receiving blanket from my own shoulder as the baby's shoulders were wriggling out of the warm refuge, and I gained a safe, gentle grip on the slick, wet babe. Though the moment was sacred and fleeting, I was able to realize and momentarily appreciate that my old, wrinkled hands were catching a newborn baby for the last time.

I immediately handed the loosely wrapped newborn up to the brand-new mother as she embraced her newest love and audibly moaned a sigh of great relief.

Her shoulders relaxed as she folded into her freshly born young, crumbling forward and weeping for joy at the beautiful sound of the baby's first cry. At last, she was holding her precious firstborn child, instinctively shushing and rocking and rubbing the baby's waxy vernix-coated skin as she held it against her own naked chest.

Samuel and I, both with tear-filled eyes, assisted AnnaRuth and the baby onto the bed where she laid back onto soft pastel pillows and then, cradling the baby in the crook of her left arm, she quickly examined the genitals before blissfully announcing,

"It's a boy! Our Elijah, Sam!"

I clapped my hands together in excitement for her as I voiced sincere congratulations. Of course, I would've had the same reaction had it been a baby girl, for my excitement was for AnnaRuth as she experienced the joyful moments of the baby's golden hour, which are surely never to be forgotten.

AnnaRuth then brought the baby up to her breast where he could smell the colostrum and see the dark brown skin of her nipple. He immediately began to suckle, sending a rush of oxytocin through AnnaRuth's bloodstream as he latched on and nursed for several profoundly intimate moments.

After fifteen minutes or so, I asked AnnaRuth if I could check on the progress of the final stage of birth — the delivery of the placenta. She'd been having some good, strong uterine contractions due to the hormones that the nursing baby was effortlessly providing. She was eager to rid her body of the afterbirth, so I gently massaged her womb from the outside as I held the limp, white umbilical cord in my other hand. With one or two more gentle spasms and a little push from AnnaRuth, the deep crimson, spongy placenta was expelled onto the towel I'd placed beneath her bottom.

With gloved hands, I swiftly unpackaged a pair of sterile scissors and a small plastic clamp, as I asked Samuel if he wanted to cut the cord which still connected baby Elijah to the powerful organ that had been his life support within the womb. Samuel was rightfully proud to sever the pair of arteries and single vein, and shortly after, he held the scales as we weighed the baby in a cotton sling. Elijah was a whopping 10 pounds, 10 ounces!

Once we'd weighed baby Elijah, he was placed back on his mother's chest where the two of them bonded in each other's warmth until well into the evening. Samuel stayed on the bed close by them, admiring his wife and new baby with wonder and excitement in his teary, joy-filled eyes.

I checked AnnaRuth's blood pressure again and then I carefully stitched up the place where she'd torn. I gently cleaned the trail of blood from AnnaRuth's legs before cleaning up the blood spill from the floor. Then, I went into the kitchen and warmed a large mug full of homemade bone broth that I'd made at home for the special purpose of nourishing the brand-new mother. While she was sipping the oily, caramel-colored broth, I took some of it from the jar and used it to make a thick soup. I'd brought fresh herbs, vegetables, and many spices, in addition to some of my home-grown beef for a delicious combination of nutrient-rich ingredients that I poured over three bowls of jasmine rice— one each for Samuel and me, as well.

Once AnnaRuth had filled her body with the warm vegetable beef soup, I took her bowl and returned with a warm bottle of avocado oil of which I'd added a few drops of pure rose oil. Then, I sat at the end of her bed and massaged her feet while she and baby Elijah rested beneath the warmth of a heavy handmade quilt. Afterwards, I placed a pair of warm fleece socks on AnnaRuth's freshly oiled feet before slowly covering them with the quilt.

Around 8 pm, when I was satisfied with both the amount of blood lost and fluids consumed, I left a small bottle of myrrh oil for baby Elijah's cord stump, and I packed my things while reminding Samuel of the fresh sourdough bread that I'd made the day before and brought along with some of Ginger's delectable butter.

The drive home was a bittersweet one. I was very much aware that I'd attended my last birth, and that fact is a bit harrowing. However, the sweet satisfaction I feel each time a baby is born in my presence was as strong as ever. In fact, it was just as strongly present as the weight of sadness I felt lingering on the surface. Even more so than ever before, as I drove down the familiar winding road amidst the tall lanky pines, I marveled at the magnificent and beautiful miracle of life.

It was twilight when I arrived back home, the frogs and crickets already singing their melodious summer song in the warmth of the dim blue evening. I sauntered slowly to the house, taking in the glorious scent of gardenias and Honey Perfume roses through the thick humid air, weighed down with both poignant thoughts and satchels of used birth supplies.

Once I had taken a shower and greased my sore knee with a generous amount of wintergreen-dandelion salve, I put away some of the tools I'd never use on a laboring mother or newborn baby again.

On the day following the birth of baby Elijah, I went straight out for a visit, following Ginger's morning milking session. I took the fresh milk along with me, for AnnaRuth and Samuel. I also took two dozen fresh eggs, and a warm French toast casserole that I'd made for them.

Both AnnaRuth and baby Elijah were thriving. AnnaRuth seemed in good spirits and did not appear to be suffering from exhaustion. I reminded her to try and stay in bed with the baby as much as possible over the next few weeks, and to make sure and keep herself warm.

Then, I returned every day for a week with a warm, hearty meal, some saffron or ginger tea, and a willingness to clean up any mess that might have naturally fallen secondary to the precious new addition to the family.

Yesterday was the last day that I'll visit, unless AnnaRuth should call upon me. I suppose that's why I've taken to journaling so relentlessly on this drizzly morning. Now, I have nothing much to do besides my usual keeping of the farm animals and the gardens. I have another two weeks before my knee operation, which I am not looking forward to very much. Madge has volunteered to look after the farm while I recover, in exchange for as much of the late crops as she can harvest before the first frost.

I'm sure to journal some over the course of my recovery. I can't promise it'll be uplifting thoughts that will fill my mind and these pages, but they'll be my deepest thoughts all the same.

I'm off now, to check the rain gauge and then I think I'll make myself a hot matcha mocha.

Thank you, for holding the last birth story.

Addie

TEN
PSALM 127:3

I woke to the sound of rain ferociously pelting my bedroom window in time with my noisy alarm. Ordinarily, I would be severely annoyed by the fact that I was required to get out of bed during such good "sleeping weather." I'd groan dramatically as I shuffled to the bathroom, dreading the wet journey to the rest home as if I were going in for a tooth extraction.

This morning, however, I feel no dread or misery. Instead, I feel ready to embrace the workday and whatever lies ahead. As I rise to a sitting position and begin to stretch my arms, the primrose diary slides down my chest and falls open onto my blanketed lap. I must've quickly drifted off to sleep after reading AnnaRuth's birth story as told by Addie. I slept so well; I don't remember dreaming a single dream or being kicked or slobbered on by Dill at all.

Maybe the deep sleep is responsible for my positive outlook on this would-be drab morning. Maybe the enchantingly satisfying story I read moments before drifting off is responsible for the quality of that sleep.

As I face myself in the mirror, waiting for the water to warm, I turn my head back and forth, angling my chin upward to the right and then to the left. I pucker my lips slightly and tousle my blonde mane, which currently looks like a mop meets a rat's nest.

I've never been a person of vanity. Confidence? Yes, but not because of my physical appearance. If anything, I've wished for stunning features like those of Jill's. Her strikingly high cheekbones, jet black hair, and natural olive skin tone are a stark contrast to my ordinary characteristics.

As I gently wipe my face with the warm washcloth, for the first time in a long time, I pay close attention to my facial features and imperfections. My nose, which turns up slightly at the tip, dotted with tiny brown freckles down the center. My eyelashes, straight as sticks, but long and wispy. Wavy horizontal creases across my forehead. A scar on my lip from a childhood injury involving barbed wire.

Once my face is moistened and refreshed, I reach into the top drawer and sift through an assortment of vitamins and hair ties until I locate what I'm searching for. My blue floral makeup bag.

I haven't worn any makeup in ages, but maybe none of it has fossilized inside the containers. I'm also just making a faithful assumption that I can even remember how to apply it.

It's almost as if I'm digging through the cosmetic-filled bag for the first time because I don't remember ever owning some of these items but apparently I've used them at some point. The small plastic containers, varying in shape and exact size are each smudged with tan powdery residue and appear to be about half used.

"This'll do," I tell myself as I set out a tube of pale concealer, a palette containing a peach-colored blush and a variety of eyeshadow tints, and a black tube of mascara which is probably caked up and dried into the bristles. Rummaging through the bag with clickety-clacking sounds in search of a couple of brushes for application, I run across a mocha tinted lip balm which I take out and add to my pile on the counter. I actually do remember that one; it smells like cocoa butter, and I bought it at the beach like a decade ago. I'm sure it's still fine, though.

"No, Dill. I wasn't calling you," I say as I face him where he lies on the bed looking curiously at me.

I find, as I work on painting the blank canvas, that applying makeup is, in fact, like riding a bicycle. Lips puckered and cheeks sucked in to apply the blush; mouth opened in a long oval shape for the mascara which is miraculously still usable. See? I've got this, I tell myself as I do some blending.

Once I'm satisfied with my fresh appearance, I grab a hairbrush from the drawer and begin to detangle the rats' nests. Should I pull my hair up into a messy knot like usual? It seems a waste of all this makeup and effort just to wear the same old hairstyle, doesn't it? It would only take a couple of minutes to run the flat iron over my fine, shoulder-length locks, I decide.

Once I'm all straightened and brushed, primped and polished, I step into the bedroom, dimly lit by the bathroom light, and take a look in the full-sized mirror that stands in the corner. My favorite choice of uniforms is normally solid black, but today I have decided to switch it up and go with the pale lilac color. The feminine lavender-ish shade of purple seems to pair pretty well with my summer sun-tinted skin.

"What has gotten into me?" Nobody is here to answer, Blaire. Dill doesn't count, and besides he's back to snoring like a hibernating grizzly bear.

As the unfamiliar and oddly attractive face in the mirror stares back at me, my eyes widen as I suddenly have the realization that Meg is going to give me heck about this. I can just hear her non-stop teasing already. A smile cracks across my dolled-up face as I step away from the mirror, prepared to defend my case when I'm inevitably scrutinized in the near future.

"Dill!" I call as I near the bed where he's stretched out. "Come on, boy. You're going to be ticked that it's raining," I mutter between clenched teeth as I playfully scratch his warm ears before forcing him outdoors to do his business in the downpour.

I feel fresh and revitalized this morning, despite the gloomy weather. Maybe I should put forth an effort to make myself look nice every day. Miraculously, I'm early today even with the time it took to apply makeup and fix my hair. With my granola bar and monogrammed mug of strong, dark roast coffee in hand, I and my giant bag and clear bubble umbrella escape the front door to greet the day.

~

In the same moment that I swiped my badge through the time clock slot this morning, the dreaded sound of a distress call echoed down the long vacant hallway. Even in the state of anguish and apparent confusion, the voice was recognized as Mr. Peterson's. He resides in room 107, and he's just about the sweetest man there ever was. Just about.

At the sound, I bolted around the corner and sprinted toward his room, the bag on my shoulder being tossed about and my warm coffee sloshing out of the sip hole. As I raced toward room 107, I saw Sharon hastily rounding the corner at the nourishment room, power-walking toward me and the destination between us, as fast as her short legs would carry her.

I veered into Mr. Peterson's room and dropped all of my belongings onto the chair by the door, before rushing to him, where he was laying sideways across his bed wildly flailing his arms and legs. I very briefly took notice of Mr. Carpenter, sitting up in his bed by the window, with his dark gray hair disheveled and a look of confusion mixed with utter displeasure in his half-opened eyes.

Mr. Peterson was yelling out words that were hard to understand, slurring, with a wild but vacant look in his eyes. I immediately darted to his nightstand and retrieved the plastic pencil box which houses his personal glucometer. I quickly shoved a test strip into it as I flopped down on the bed and reached for his clammy hand. I skipped the alcohol pad and went straight for the lancet.

"Mr. Peterson," I said calmly. "Shhh… Mr. Peterson, it's okay. Let's check your blood sugar, alright?" He didn't realize he was being spoken to, let alone comprehend what I was saying to him. I somehow managed to get a drop of his blood onto the test strip sticking out of the glucometer, despite his active flailing. Right about that time, Sharon entered the room, short of breath and wide-eyed.

Beeeeep. The glucometer read 19 mg/dL.

"I'll get the glucagon," I said breathlessly as I held up the glucometer for Sharon to see.

"Can I have the keys?" I held out my hand, adrenaline and caffeine pulsing through my veins like hot lava and making me jittery. Somehow, it didn't feel stressful. Instead, it felt invigorating.

She took her hand from her chest and hurriedly rummaged through her shirt pocket before producing a large ring full of keys and handing it to me as I raced out of the room toward the medication stock room.

Once I'd given Mr. Peterson the shot in his upper arm, he was conscious, and I was confident that he was on his way to a complete recovery, I left him alone in bed and went with Sharon to the nurses' station to receive the night's shift report, which was otherwise uneventful. I told her not to worry about the legal portion of Mr. Peterson's crisis. "I'll take care of the paperwork," I said with a wave as we finished up the narcotic count. She didn't hesitate to gather her belongings and head straight for the time clock as she bid her farewell to me and Sunny Grove "for the next four days, thank the Lord!" Sharon was happy to report that she and her husband were going out of town for the apple festival.

After the shift report, I headed straight back to check on Mr. Peterson, who was propped up in bed watching the local news channel and washing peanut butter crackers down with sips of 7UP.

"How are you feeling?" I asked as I popped my head in the doorway.

"A little weak, but I'm alright darling," he said quietly beneath the sound of the TV and Mr. Carpenter's bear-like snoring. He sure made a loud noise for such a little man.

I stepped into the room and walked over to Mr. Peterson's bedside. I felt his forehead, which felt warm and dry.

"I'll call your son and tell him what happened as soon as I get back up to the nurses' station," I told him.

"Oh, you ain't gotta call him," Mr. Peterson assured me as he gave a wave of disregard.

"You know I've got to," I reminded him with a teasing tone.

"Just like I had to call and let him know I put this Band-Aid here on your arm yesterday," I pointed out as I grazed the tiny bandage on his left forearm. Underneath it, is the superficial break in the skin left by Mr. Peterson himself, scratching at an itchy spot while sleeping. It does seem absurd, but policy states that I must notify the family of the patient for any and all treatment measures. The intervention for that incident was, of course, to trim his fingernails.

He shook his head at this. "Hey, Lordy, I declare," he slowly sang with a half chuckle."Do they think you've got nothing else to do?"

I laughed and agreed with him before reaching for the glucometer to check his blood sugar once more, which had increased to 88 mg/dL.

"Don't you scare me like that again, you hear?" I teased only to let him know I cared enough to worry about him. I know that it wasn't anything he'd done. In fact, the nursing staff on the night shift are supposed to ensure that he gets a snack at midnight, and I'd be willing to bet that it slipped all of their minds.

He snickered at my request. "I'll try not to," he promised in a hushed voice.

Once Mr. Peterson was stable, I called for Meg and asked her to go ahead and retrieve his breakfast tray early. Surprisingly, she didn't give me a hard time about my being all dolled up, though it wasn't a concern of mine at the time.

I called Mr. Peterson's son and explained the morning's events before loading up my cart with puddings and purées and beginning the monumental med pass.

I guess you could say that Mr. Peterson basically crashing sort of set the tone for the rest of the day, because from then onward, the day was filled with events that needed my attention. Somehow, though, I've remained calm, and I even managed to eat a package of peanuts and a Little Debbie cake that I swiped from the resident snack cart that was brought up by the dietary staff.

No sooner than I'd finished the morning round passing out all of the medications, I heard Mrs. Colter yelling for help. Which, of course, meant she was lying on the floor because she'd temporarily forgotten she'd long ago lost the use of her legs as well as her bladder and she tried to go to the restroom. Between the muscle weakness and the catheter bag being attached to the undercarriage of her wheelchair, she wound up in a prone position on the floor of her room, tied to her wheelchair by a bag of urine. She was uninjured, thank the Lord.

I decided to bring her along with me for a while as I completed the pressing tasks of the day, so that I could keep an eye on her and make sure she didn't develop a delayed response to the fall. She made good company for me in the nurses' station, while I completed paperwork, and she folded some washcloths I snagged from the laundry room on the way back up.

Later, Mr. Carpenter pulled the fire alarm which sent the whole building into a panicked tizzy, and after that Ms. Ethel had a catastrophic event involving her colostomy bag, which resulted in a shower, a complete change of bed linens, total reconstruction of the colostomy appliance, and two Imodium tablets.

I've had far worse workdays in terms of actual crises rather than inconvenient obstacles, but I'm beginning to feel the burn of a tired back, and I know I'll rest well tonight.

While Ann, the Director of Nursing, was supervising breakfast in the residents' dining room this morning, I went ahead and requested some time off so that I can start moving as soon as the closing is completed. Counting the next two days which are my scheduled days off, I'll have a grand total of fourteen days off. I've never taken nearly that much time since I started nursing, and while I'm not as anxious as Sharon is to be away from The Home, I'm positively euphoric about the upcoming move into the farmhouse. Though I've been too busy to think much about it today, the exciting thoughts linger in the back of my mind constantly, sort of teasing me and giving the workday little trills that ease the thick of the challenges.

Now, as I sit in the quiet confines of the homey nurses' station, I feel the soft touch of someone gently combing my hair with their fingers.

"You look pretty today, Blaire," sings Meg as she continues to slowly tousle my rarely straightened hair, her fingers softly grazing my tired shoulders, sending chills down my spine.

"Oh, thanks," I reply without looking up from Ms. Ethel's chart which lies open on my lap.

"I don't think I've ever seen you with your hair down," Meg continues. "And that lavender color looks great on you!"

I know where this conversation is headed, and I'm not sure if I can avoid it unless another catastrophe happens to break loose right at this very moment.

"Yeah, I know. I just felt like fixing myself up a little bit today. You know, it gets kind of old looking so blah all the time," I explain as I continue to make notes in Ms. Ethel's chart, my back still toward Meg.

"Yeah, I know what you mean," she replies with a sarcastic kind of tone before leaning over my shoulder.

Then she continues in a hushed tone, "I thought you might like to know that the cute policeman is in Mrs. Simms' room."

I abruptly stop filling out Ms. Ethel's pain assessment sheet and I feel my stomach seize and clinch as my heart picks up the pace of a locomotive.

"Oh, yeah?" I quickly begin writing again although it's a mindless scribble that I'll need to proofread before leaving it in the incident report folder.

"Yeah. I thought I heard him say something about needing to talk to the nurse. I'm not sure what abou —"

We both catch a glimpse of someone approaching the nurses' station at exactly the same second. Wearing his black uniform and shiny badge, he's headed down the corridor straight for the door that leads into the small room where Meg and I are fervently trying to look as though we're totally immersed in other affairs.

When he reaches the point where even an honestly oblivious Blaire couldn't miss him in her peripheral vision, I look up from my stack of papers and make eye contact with him.

"Oh, hey!" I greet him enthusiastically, pretending I'm just noticing him now.

"Hey, there," he replies with a smile as real as the sea as he stops just short of the doorway into the nurses' station. I notice a toothpick sticking out of the left side of his mouth.

"Do you need something?" I ask, turning toward him in the swivel chair and setting aside the random assortment of papers that belong in the shred box.

"Well," he begins.

"First of all, shame on you for lying to me. Telling me you've 'never heard of' a Mrs. Margaret Simms," he scoffs teasingly as he shakes his head back and forth.

"Hey, I *hadn't* ever heard of a Mrs. Margaret Simms, until about two hours after you came looking for her!" I playfully retort in defense.

"I know, I know. I'm messing with you," he assures me with a grin, as our eyes lock. I know he's only joking, but without pointless arguments there would only be awkwardness.

Then he continues. "No, actually Mrs. Margaret said she would sure like to have a cold Coke," he explains in a sort of abashed fashion.

"She said she hasn't had any since before she went into the hospital and she's got a hankering for some. I'll buy her one, but I didn't know if she should drink it or not. I sure don't want to give her something that she's not supposed to have."

Well, if that isn't the sweetest thing.

"I don't *think* she has any restrictions, but let me double check to be sure." I reach for Mrs. Simms' burgundy plastic chart which is void of the pale blue sticker on the spine that indicates diabetes. I admitted her, I care for and administer her medications almost daily. I know she's not a diabetic, or at least she has no diagnosis of diabetes, and I know she doesn't receive thickened liquids due to any sort of swallowing difficulty.

But, if I give him the go-ahead right away, I risk his immediate retreat to oblige Mrs. Margaret's request.

Flipping to her "face sheet", I glance down at the opened chart on my lap.

"Oh yeah, she's good." I nod as I look up at Joseph.

But he doesn't immediately retreat to fill the lady's simple request. Instead, he leans his body against the door jamb and I purposefully withhold information on the location of the vending machines.

I take notice of Meg escaping outside to the wooden stair landing where she will soon fill her lungs with the smoke from an ignited Marlboro menthol ultralight. When I'm not busy, I'll sometimes take a break with her while the familiar cigarette smoke and memories of Daddy both swirl thickly around me. It takes me back to the days of young Blaire sitting in the passenger seat of Daddy's old blue Ford pickup, toking a long cigarette while listening to Roy Acuff on cassette tapes.

"How's your day been?" Joseph asks, still standing in the doorway.

"Very busy," I proclaim with wide eyes as I place Mrs. Margaret's chart back in its place on the wooden rack.

"How about yours?" I ask.

"My workday is just starting. I go in on the *night* shift," he replies with a bit of a frown.

"I see. I take it you don't care for nights?"

"Oh, it's alright," he says with a wave. "Somebody's gotta do it, right?"

He chews on the toothpick, sharpening his defined jawline and revealing strong facial muscles.

"Yeah, I know what you mean," I chuckle, empathetic to the second half of his comment.

"Well," Joseph begins as he looks down and kicks one black leather boot with the other.

"I guess I'd better get back to Mrs. Margaret with that drink."

Just as I'm about to disclose the directions to the vending machine, the outside door behind me opens and Jill emerges carrying her large satchel, bringing with her the remnants of Meg's smoke break.

"Hey, hey!" I greet Jill excitedly. I'd lost track of time and failed to realize it's already five minutes until seven.

"Hola," she answers as she looks over toward Joseph and back at me.

"What's happening today?" she asks.

"Everything!" I snicker. "But it's all under control now."

"This is Joseph," I explain as I nod toward him. "He's visiting Mrs. Simms."

"I'm Jill," she informs him happily. "I'll be the nurse tonight. Are you a family member, or…?"

"No ma'am, just a friend. I go to church with Mrs. Margaret, and I stopped by to pay her a visit on my way to work tonight," he explains.

"Ah, the good old night shift," Jill says with a grin as she raises a green bottle of Sundrop and sits her bag on the long wooden table.

"Yeah," Joseph agrees with a chuckle.

Then, as he pushes himself from the door jamb and stands upright, "Well, I'll be going now, so y'all can get back to your work. You ladies have a good night."

He takes the chewed-up toothpick from between his teeth and throws his hand up as he walks backwards toward the hallway outside the nurses' station.

"You too. Don't work too hard!" Jill calls.

Before turning his back to Jill and I, Joseph locks eyes with me and winks, while flashing a bright toothy smile.

I watch him round the corner and disappear to the right, next to the vending area. I guess he figured out where it was located on his own. No way possible the hum or the glow of the machines gave any clue.

"Blaire??" Jill prods, playful but with an expression of genuine curiosity.

"What?" I ask, as I busily place various documents in their appropriate places.

"Aren't I your best friend?" she asks.

"Of course," I answer dryly without bothering to ask the reason for her question.

"Whom you tell everything to, correct?"

"Yep. I sure do," I confirm.

"Well, then why didn't you tell me you met a man?" Jill demands, though I can hear the hint of a smile in her voice.

Finally, I look up at Jill to see her arms folded across her chest and her lips in a wide, thin smirk.

"What do you mean, 'met a man'? The guy just came in to visit a patient, and then you came in. How could I have told you anything? As if there was anything to tell," I quickly add.

"Oh, no no. Don't play dumb with me, Blaire," Jill retorts. "We've worked here for five years, and you've *never* worn your hair down or a single drop of makeup to work. All of a sudden you do both, and then what to my wondering eyes should appear but a very handsome young man void of a wedding band standing in the nurses' station alone with you. Hmmm…" she taps her index finger on her chin pretending to deeply ponder my sudden peculiarity.

"Oh, whatever. You and Meg are *killing* me, accusing me of…what? I don't even know!" I exclaim in a whispered tone, aware that Joseph could stop back by.

"Blaire." Jill sits in the swivel chair and looks at me with wide eyes and a wider smile. "It's okay! It's more than okay. But I'm going to need the details as soon as you're ready, alright?"

This cracks me up. "Okay, Jill. I'll give you the details. He came in yesterday looking for Mrs. Simms, and she wasn't here yet, so he undoubtedly came back today. End of story."

"Mmhm, I don't know if I buy it," Jill says.

"Well, that's *it*." I argue, stamping my foot.

"Alright, alright. Well, just let me know if there are any developments or anything, *okay*?" She asks, persistent.

"Okay," I agree, a bit sarcastic. "Can we do report now? Today has been kind of a beast."

"Sure. I can't wait," Jill answers.

"Oh, and guess what," I say gleefully. "I'm now off for two weeks!"

"What?" Jill asks, shocked.

"Yeah, I talked to Ann today and she said that Jaime, that part-time nurse, really needed some hours and she's going to fill in for me. So, it works out really well, and that'll give me plenty of time to get all moved and settled in," I explain, wearing a satisfied smile.

"Wow, that's exciting!" Jill agrees. "I'll miss you here, though. I can't wait to be off for a couple of days, that way Todd and I can help you move," she says.

"Well, I don't have *that* much stuff. So maybe it won't be so bad," I shrug.

"Keep me informed," Jill requests as she holds her hand out for the med-cart keys. "Now let's get these narcotics counted, so you can get home. You're closing on the house tomorrow, right?" Jill asks excitedly.

"I am." I smile with satisfaction as I dangle the nurse keys between Jill and I.

ELEVEN
SONG OF SONGS 2:11-12

After I gave Jill the run-down of all the day's happenings and made her responsible for any more that may occur, I hung around for just a little while. Of course, Jill thought it was to catch a glimpse of Joseph, but honestly I just wasn't in any hurry to leave tonight. I guess the fact that I won't see the place for two weeks made me feel like staying a bit longer.

I tied up a few loose ends; little things I'd been neglecting the past few shifts such as behavior charting and recording all of the latest vital signs in the patients' charts. I stood by the medicine cart and talked with Jill while she made her round passing out the bedtime medications. Then suddenly, while in mid-sentence about the offensively loud volume of Miss Cathy's TV, Addie flashed to the forefront of my thoughts. Another happy undertone that's surely been beneath the surface of my preoccupied mind all day, silently propelling me in a direction of positivity and peacefulness.

Once I had the satisfying epiphany, I quickly decided it was time to say goodbye to Jill and gather my things. I didn't see Joseph anymore; I assume he left before I did, to begin his shift. `

On the drive home, I cracked the window and enjoyed the crispness of an early fall. The sun had just dipped behind the mountains ahead when I got on the highway toward home, which eliminated the necessity for my sunglasses, but I continued to wear them anyway.

Dill was most anxious to receive me back home, more to relieve himself than to receive my presence. I apologized to him for being late and thanked him for not using the bathroom on the floor. Although, I wouldn't have scolded him even if he had. It's not his fault I'm late.

I unpacked my lunchbox and then Dill and I headed down the hall where I had a quicker than usual bath, but one that left me feeling free from nursing home grime.

Now, as I stand in the bedroom wearing an old cotton tee-shirt, I'm drawing a blank as to where Addie's diary could be. I had it this morning, right? It was on the bed the last time I saw it, but now it's nowhere to be found.

"Dill, where's that diary? You know, the one with the pretty pink and yellow flowers on it?"

"Oh, a lot of help you are," I mumble as I fluff the pillows, checking underneath them again.

It can't be far away; I had it *right here* just this morning. I know I didn't put it in my work bag, but I suppose I'll check there anyway.

To the kitchen I trudge, to remove everything from the large bag in an attempt to locate the missing diary.

As I step into the living room, I hear the muffled sound of my phone ringing. I glance at the clock on the mantle and wonder who would be calling me at 9 o' clock. It could be Jill, either asking me a question about one of the residents or relaying a message from one of them, as she often does.

I pick up the pace and follow the sound to my bag by the dining table, Dill right on my heels the whole way. I reach in and scramble to find the ringing phone. Finally, I manage to find and retrieve it while it's still playing its loud musical tone.

But, when I look at the screen, it's not Jill or the number for The Home. Instead, it's a number I don't know, but I do recognize the area code as being one from Bascomb County.

"Hmm," I say aloud. I suppose it could be the realtor calling from a different number. He's about the only person I know from up that way.

I tap the glass screen and bring the phone to my ear.

"Hello?" I answer.

In response, I hear the recognizable voice that, with just one word, sends my heart into immediate tachycardia and a dozen hummingbirds into my stomach.

"Hey," is all he says.

"Hey, yourself," I reply, unable to control the nervousness.

"I hope you don't mind, but I asked Meg for your number," he says.

"I knew it had to be either Meg or Jill." I giggle.

"And no, I don't mind, but why didn't you just ask *me*?"

"Well, I would've, eventually. But she basically offered it to me, to be honest. And I wasn't going to turn it down," he says with a snicker.

"So, what are you up to?"

"That Meg, I swear," I reply, although I secretly feel like hugging her.

"But I'm not doing much. Just getting ready for bed, soon. Aren't you supposed to be working?" I prod.

"Well, yes." he chuckles. I'm on patrol tonight and there's not much happening right now."

"I see," I reply, pacing the short length across the kitchen floor and back.

"Do you work tomorrow?" Joseph asks.

"No, actually I'm off for two weeks as of 7 o'clock tonight," I boldly proclaim.

"Two weeks? Are you going somewhere?" he questions.

"Oh, just to my new house," I answer.

"You're moving, I see," he states the obvious."Where to? If you don't mind me asking," he quickly adds.

"Not too far. I just bought an old house in the country, in Bascomb."

"Oh really?" he asks. "I live in Bascomb."

"Nice! How do you like it there? I've always lived in Weatherford."

"I've always called Bascomb home, so I've got nothing to compare it to," he replies.

Home. I hang onto that word, pondering it. It perfectly describes what I so desperately hope for in the farmhouse. Comfort and contentment experienced within the walls of a space seasoned with love and attention. Maybe even loved ones to share it with.

Having a family in that house is something I can see clearly, but I wonder if I'll ever be able to grasp it. It may always be out of my reach, but the desire in my heart for it bubbles over and burns with a sad, yearning sting.

I truly can't imagine anything more wonderful than building a happy life and raising children with the husband of my dreams. I can't imagine having someone to come home to.

I'd be the mother I never had. I'd cook the way Grandmama did, rising early to put hot biscuits and gravy in the middle of a large oak dining table that sits at least ten. I'd kiss bee stings and bandage skinned knees. I'd never complain about a single thing, ever again. Will I ever have that, I wonder, or will it always be a far-fetched dream?

Thinking of that life brings tears to my tired eyes as I lay in bed, euphoric about the three-hour-long conversation Joseph and I had tonight. He had to hang up and call me back twice to attend to his job, but during the time that we talked, we learned a lot about each other.

I learned that he's six years older than I am, he's a deputy for Bascomb County and has been for the past seven years. He and his bloodhound named Tucker live alone, also in the country and only about ten minutes from the farmhouse.

He knows I don't have any family, but I didn't crack open the empty vault that stands in the center of my heart, representing the hopeless sorrow that's the result of losing the only people whom I ever loved. The only people who ever loved me.

On the contrary, Joseph's parents are both alive and well. He has two brothers, and a grandpa whom he treasures. He spends every Sunday afternoon in the presence of all of them, surrounding the dining table at his Mama's house. I briefly burned with envy as he talked about this, but the sting was soothed by the satisfaction of knowing such wonderful things do exist.

As I lay in the still of the late night, I think of Addie. Her apparent joy despite the anguish that lies beneath it; her ability to gracefully drown out the loneliness with motivation to serve others and a will to thrive. I admit that she's taken the backseat compared to the meeting of Joseph and the fast-approaching date that I'll finally be moving into my dream home. But I'm keeping her close, in my back pocket, for a time in which the events of my life simmer down a bit and I can fully enjoy her words for all they're worth. I'm certain I'll need them to comfort the ache of my fractured heart as the days grow colder and darker. Or, as I'm feeling the sting of solitude without even the company of my patients or coworkers over the next two weeks.

I found Addie's floral notebook on the floor between my bed and the wall, as I was straightening up the sheets before climbing into bed tonight. I picked it up and laid it on my nightstand in plain sight, where it will remain safe until I can savor it with complete mindfulness.

Right now, I can't focus on anything except the wonderfully exciting day that lies ahead of me. In the morning, I will go down to the lawyer's office and finally sign the closing paperwork for *my house*. I smile to myself as I think of those words while picturing the farmhouse that will belong to me in less than twelve hours.

Beyond that, are the plans Joseph and I have made to spend the evening at the Bascomb County fair. We agreed that it would make a fun first date. I must admit, though; when Joseph first mentioned it, my heart became heavy and sank for a moment as I felt the pang of nostalgia. I haven't been to the fair since I was about thirteen years old. Being back in a place that I haven't visited since I was there with Daddy is sure to jab at the tender emotions that haven't even begun to heal.

This morning when I began my day, I was just hoping I might catch a glimpse of Joseph sometime while doling out medications. I never imagined we'd spend half the night talking on the phone and planning a date for the following evening.

I warned him of my rustiness in the dating world. I haven't dated since a very brief fling during nursing school and until now, I haven't met a guy with manners or morals that I'm willing to accept. I knew right away that Joseph was different from the other guys I've met. His attitude, his language, the fact that he looked at my face instead of my body. I realize I don't know him well enough to have a fully developed opinion of him, but so far, he's an exception to today's pitiful expectations and that gives him an A+ in my book.

Joseph told me that he hasn't had a girlfriend in two years, himself. He didn't go into details about any past relationships, but then I wouldn't expect him to.

He's supposed to pick me up at 6 o' clock tomorrow evening. As the hour approaches, I'm sure nervousness will creep in but right now, I'm nothing but giddy.

The adrenaline coursing through my body and the thoughts racing about my mind won't quite allow me to surrender to the exhaustion I'd otherwise feel.

I pick up my phone from its place next to Addie's diary and check the time. 2:17 AM. I've been awake for almost twenty-one hours, and I worked my tail off at The Home for the majority of those.

As I still my body, my head resting on the satin pillow and Dill snoring rhythmically beside me, warmth radiating from his soft curls, I finally begin to feel the dire need for sleep. I recognize my body slowing its pace and relaxing in preparation for a deep, restful slumber. Peace and serenity blanket me with a thick, heavy warmth as visions of carousels and ferris wheels twirl and spin just beneath my heavy eyelids.

TWELVE
Isaiah 9:6

"Popular place tonight, huh?" Joseph's deep voice seems to vibrate off my clammy skin as I sit in the shotgun seat of his Chevy Silverado.

"Yeah, it sure is," I agree. "It's the first night of the fair for this year, I think."

"Oh, yeah. Well, that would be why, wouldn't it?" He grips the steering wheel. "But we're in no hurry, are we?" He gives me a sideways glance, partnered with that charming half-smile he wears so well.

"Not at all." I give him an assuring smile. "I don't have to be up early for the next two weeks!" I declare, maybe too excitedly.

"That's right. It must be nice…" Joseph teases with a chuckle as we inch our way toward the gates of the county fair.

"Yeah, it is," I agree. "But it feels very odd. I've never been away from the place for that long before. I'll definitely miss my residents."

"Well, it's a much-deserved break, then. You'll have plenty to keep busy with the move, though," he says.

"I know," I agree. "In a good way though. I can't wait to be in the new house. The new *old* house, that is."

"I wish I could picture where it is," he says. "I looked up the address so I know it's not far from me but I can't recall ever having gone down that road before."

"Well, maybe you can see it soon," I hint, hopeful to the brim.

I suppose that all depends on how the evening fairs. No pun intended.

"Yeah, surely I will," he says with a trickle of a smile as we find our parking spot in the grass between two poorly parked vehicles.

"People around here are excellent drivers," Joseph comments sarcastically as he pulls the truck snugly between the two. "Trust me on that one," he adds.

"Oh yeah, I bet you run into all kinds of kinds, don't you?" I laugh.

He gives me a wide-eyed glare. "You don't know the half of it, and don't wanna," he says, shaking his head.

"Stay put," he says as he unlatches the driver door. I'm going to squeeze my way over there and open your door for you."

Inside the gates of the noisy fairgrounds, the smell of deep-fried corn dogs, breaded onions, and Oreos fill my fragile senses and nostalgia pours over and drenches me. The aroma paired with the flashing colors of the many rides and booths take me right back to the days of my tender youth.

"How many tickets do you want for the rides?"

Joseph's words suddenly bring me back to the present and I'm reminded that I'm no longer a twelve-year-old girl wandering through the crowd, euphoric, while my daddy shows his steer in the livestock competition.

"Oh, goodness!It's been so long since I've ridden any sort of ride," I confess with an embarrassed snicker. Mostly embarrassed by the realization that I'm not a young girl anymore.

"Well, me too but I'll buy as many as you want," he offers, pulling his wallet from the back pocket of his jeans.

Through the thick crowd of Bascomb County folks and swirls of Marlboro smoke, we wind around until we find the food vendors least likely to give us botulism.

"Barbeque sound good?" He asks as we approach a food truck with scrumptious-smelling smoke billowing from it.

"Or we can keep walking. It's up to you," he offers.

"Sounds just perfect to me. I'm starving," I admit as we pin ourselves to the tail end of the line.

Fellow fair goers surround us, sucking ears of corn on the cob, a cigarette, or both. Sounds of sizzling junk foods, games and squeals from those on the rickety rides fill the air so that Joseph and I have to speak loudly to be heard by one another.

"I'm hungry myself," he says, leaning closer to me. "If I'm being honest, the food is the only thing I've ever enjoyed about the fair." he snickers.

"Oh, really? You mean you don't enjoy the mass of people trying to fit into your pocket or the pop-up rides or the secondhand smoke from cigarettes and possibly other plant products?"

He laughs at this. "No, I'm enjoying it all," he says. "Tonight, anyway."

And for the first time, he puts his arm around my waist and gently pulls me closer to him.

My heart begins to flutter as our hips briefly press against each other and I wonder if he notices my cheeks flushing or the sweat beginning to bead above my brows.

It takes a good long while of standing in line before we reach the front, but neither of us mind. The sun has slowly sunk, turning the orangey pink autumn sky pitch black, dotted with glittery stars. Likewise, thousands of colorful lights twinkle around us, illuminating the night air with the flashing bulbs of carousels and concession stands.

We found a small, splintery table in the corner of the covered area by the barbecue stand where we sat and devoured sandwiches and onion rings through laughter, tears included. I haven't cried as the result of laughter since I was a teenage girl. It feels absolutely freeing, but simultaneously a little frightening.

What if this is a one-time date, and I return to my normal life in a couple weeks like nothing ever happened except that I'm living in a new home? I'll have had one evening of bliss tucked in among years of melancholy-drenched monotony.

"I'll admit, I was nervous about how I'd feel being back here after all these years," I confess from across the table.

"Really?" Joseph asks, perplexed.

"Yeah. I was afraid it would bring back all sorts of childhood memories, reminding me that I'm an orphan and that my daddy is never coming back." I wipe imaginary crumbs from my lap.

Joseph looks tenderly at me, compassion deep within his light brown eyes.

"When I was little, we came here every fall. Daddy always entered livestock in the competitions, and I just had so much fun, walking around with friends, without a care in the world."

"I guess you could say I was in my Fern Arable era." I laugh, rebuking the threat of tears.

"Surprisingly, I do know who Fern Arable is, thanks to my fifth-grade teacher, Mrs. Reese," he says proudly.

"Oh, wow. Well, you just get better all the time." I smile, wondering to myself where the confidence to be flirtatious with him has come from.

"Is that right?" Joseph asks, a bit playfully.

"That's right," I reply, leaning toward him.

He reaches across the table and gently takes both my hands in his as the hummingbirds return to my stomach.

Suddenly we both become aware that most of the tables surrounding us have become vacant.

"Well." Joseph says, looking over his shoulder.

"How long have we been sitting here? The supper crowd has died out." he laughs.

"I don't even know," I reply honestly. "You did say that you only come to the fair for the food. You ready to take me home?" I ask.

"Shoot, no," he says, smiling as he shakes his cup of ice. "I'm ready to go see the fattest pig in Bascomb county."

I laugh as I begin clearing away bits of checkered waxed paper and remnants of cold onion rings from the table.

"It's chilly tonight," I comment as we weave our way through the thick crowd. I thrust my hands into the pockets of my cardigan and pull it tightly around me as a shiver ripples across my shoulders.

I feel his giant warm hand on my back, the heat from it radiating to the rest of my body. And just that fast, I don't feel the least bit cold anymore.

"Want to ride?" He asks.

I turn to look at him and find that he's looking up at the iconic ferris wheel towering over us with a rainbow of lights illuminating it for all to see. Somehow, I had walked right up to it and hadn't even noticed the showcase of the whole event, the giant ring of flashing lights rotating with gleeful riders hanging from it.

Pulling two paper tickets from his front pocket, he says "I got these two, just for the ferris wheel." He gives me a sheepish kind of look, awaiting my response.

"Well, duh I want to ride the ferris wheel!" I answer. "It's only been like twenty years since I've ridden one of these things." That makes me sound so old.

"It hasn't been all *that* long, has it?" he asks, skeptical.

"Oh yeah, every bit of it. I sound like an old lady, don't I?"

"Nah," he says as we climb up onto the platform and head toward the next available seat.

"Are you having fun?" Joseph asks once we're well on our way up to the top of the ferris wheel, stopping frequently for additional passengers.

"I haven't had this much fun in years," I reply honestly. "And I realize how lame that sounds, but it's true that I'm really a very boring person," I confess.

"Boring," he scoffs. "Yeah, you're far from boring. I promise you that."

"No, really. My life is dull. Allow me to let you in on the most exciting part of my current life, and then you can decide whether or not I'm boring."

"Okay, I'm all ears," he says.

"Okay, so just last week, I was shopping at an antique store, right?"

I continue without his answer. "And I found a really nice old end table that I wanted for the new house for a steal of a deal. And even though the drawer was really tight, I bought it; I figured I could work it open with some elbow grease. Well, I did get it open eventually, and I found this *diary* inside."

He looks at me intently but with skepticism, still waiting for me to explain how boring I am.

"And as it turns out," I continue, "it belonged to a midwife named Addie. Oh, my goodness, she is wonderful. She has a farm where she milks her cow, she makes homemade bread and butter and all these things for the mothers she takes care of. It's kind of funny; she even goes off on a total rant about hospital births, but even that was so interesting. It doesn't even seem like real life, does it?"

"That's pretty neat. Is it old?" Joseph asks.

"It doesn't *seem* old. I mean, the pages aren't yellowed and the diary is in good condition, but there's really not been any indication of an actual timeframe. She doesn't mention anything that could hint at her whereabouts. Now, I haven't skipped ahead because I'm enjoying it *so* much and I don't want to spoil anything. I mean, it's like a story book. But I called the place where I bought the table from — *Bobbie's* — and she had no idea. She couldn't remember where the table came from or how long she'd had it, or anything. I've been so invested in Addie's life, too. But I've sort of placed her on the back burner for the moment, until I get moved in. I figure her words will really be appreciated on late nights alone in that big, new place. You know what I mean?"

I stop for air and give Joseph a chance to speak.

"Yeah, I know what you mean," he says with a grin.

"Don't make fun. I told you my life was dull," I reply.

"Oh, I'm not making fun," he assures me. "It's just kind of cute how excited you are about this."

Then he continues, "But I could check the database for you at work tomorrow night. See what comes up for the name Addie in surrounding counties, if you want."

"You *can*?!" My heart rate spikes. I'm suddenly absolutely stoked at the possibility that I may be able to find Addie.

"Oh man, that would be *amazing*, if I found her. I'm not even finished reading about her yet, but I absolutely love her. I have to meet her," I beg.

"Well, I can't make any promises. I mean, all I have to work with right now is a first name." He chuckles. "She could live anywhere. But I will try my best," he promises.

"Thank you! Oh my gosh, thank you! I can't believe this. You know, it's not too likely that she lives far away. Possible, but unlikely. Bobbie likes to shop locally. But…she does take donations," I say quietly, remembering this fact.

"I'll be letting you know what I come up with," he promises, as he slides his body against mine and wraps his arm snugly around my shoulders.

I lean into his warmth and lay my head on his shoulder, realizing that his promises to help me must mean that he wants to see me again.

Sitting at the very top of the ferris wheel, I feel like a capsule of warmth in the crisp night air, as I reflect on the girl I was and the woman I am. For the first time in my adult life, looking back doesn't hurt. Maybe it's because I now have some things to look forward to. Maybe it's because through both Joseph and Addie, I've been able to experience healing.

The feelings of euphoria that accompany these satisfying thoughts, combined with the motions from the ferris wheel have my head spinning like the musical carousel below us. The next thing I know, I'm met with the greasy, long-haired guy who's waiting for us to exit the ride.

As we step down from the small swiveling bucket, Joseph takes my hand in his, thankfully. I steady myself, but he doesn't let go. We make our way back through the crowd and toward the parking area, my hand fitting snugly in the palm of his, large and calloused. It feels as though the noise and chaos surrounding us are now muted, like everyone else is in a slow, separate space, allowing us to pass through before they carry on with their own affairs.

"You have big plans for tomorrow?" Joseph asks as he hands me a giant bagful of pink and blue cotton candy from the concession stand we've stopped in front of.

"Yeah, it's Moving Day. Didn't you know?!" I almost shout as I take a bite of the delicious spun sugar.

"Oh you're starting to move *tomorrow?* I guess I didn't realize that," he admits. "I'm sorry."

"Oh yeah, the house is mine as of this morning at 10 A.M." I declare. "I'm all packed up, and tomorrow morning my car is going to be filled to possibly an unsafe level — oh, pretend I didn't say that, officer — "

He shakes his head and smiles as he takes a bite a of cotton candy.

"And I'll be making trips back and forth all day. I'm counting on it taking a couple of days to get everything moved. I guess I should have rented a U-Haul, but that would have been too easy," I say, silently wondering why in the world I *didn't* think to rent a U-Haul.

"You don't have *anybody* to help you?" he asks.

"Well, Jill and her husband will help some. But she's working tonight, and tomorrow night. The earliest the two of them will be free to help, is like…Tuesday, I think. So, I won't move the big things, like furniture, until then. But the appliances belong to the landlord, so it's basically just my bed, a book shelf, and some smaller furniture."

"I'll just be so happy to move in. I've waited for this day for what seems like forever," I add.

"I'll bet," he says. "So, do you already have a fridge, washing machine, and dryer for the new house?"

"Yep, they're all ordered and supposed to be delivered on Monday. I also ordered a new couch, and my landlord said I could leave my old one," I answer as we slowly make our way toward the parking area.

"Well, I'm happy for you. It sounds like it's going to be a nice change," he says.

"I think so too."

It doesn't seem like a long enough ride back to my house, despite the multitude of others attempting to get home from the fair. As we pull in, I think of Dill inside the house, patiently waiting for my return. He sure is going to be confused tomorrow, when I start emptying the house of our belongings.

"Well, here we are," Joseph states the obvious as he puts the truck in park.

"I really had a lot of fun tonight," I say.

"So did I," Joseph replies. I can tell he is facing me in the darkness.

"I told you I haven't dated or anything, in forever. I'm sorry if I've been too bold, or too...anything. I don't know, I just feel like in this season of my life, I don't have it in me to put up any sort of front for impressions' sake. You know what I mean?"

Joseph laughs softly. "Blaire, I *like you*. Just how you are. Don't ever put up a front for me. Please."

His words are comforting, like a salve, adding another layer of hope. Hope for the possibility of a future relationship. And hope that I'm inching toward complete healing.

"Thank you for tonight. I truly needed it," I say.

"Don't thank me. I needed it just as much as you did, I'm sure."

"Well, I don't want to, but I guess I'd better get in. I need to let my dog out and get ready for tomorrow." I find it hard to contain my excitement.

"Let me walk you to the door," he says as he unlatches his door and quickly comes around to mine.

"Oh, you're such a gentleman." I comment playfully as I step out of the truck.

"I'll always treat you like the lady that you are," Joseph replies.

We said goodnight with a long embrace that warmed my soul the way nothing ever has before. I have resisted hugs or any form of affection from others for most of my adult life. It was such a habit that it had become a part of me, a personality quirk of sorts. A rigid, hard reality of who I was.

But, tonight, it's as if the wall I'd put up was made of a thick, hard wax all along. I imagine it melting in the warmth between Joseph and I, drops of wax trickling and puddling as the wall gets smaller and smaller.

I'd be content to stay here, wrapped in his arms until sun-up and beyond, but we eventually and reluctantly break apart and slowly walk hand-in-hand to my front door.

"Well, goodnight, Blaire," he says with one more soft squeeze around my shoulders, careful not to cross any boundaries or invite himself in.

"Oh, by the way…" he adds. "I'll be here first thing in the morning, ready to load down the ole Chevy."

"What?" I ask, surprised.

"Well, you need some help, don't you?" He starts walking down the steps and toward the truck. "Call me when you wake up, will you?"

"Okay! I will. And don't worry… I'm not getting up before the sun," I yell out into the front yard.

Before opening the door to his truck, he calls back in the dimly lit driveway, "It doesn't matter what time it is… just call me when you're ready."

And before I know it, he's slowly backing his truck out of my driveway as I stand by my front door, my sweater drawn snugly around me while I watch him leave.

THIRTEEN
ROMANS 5:3

I woke up an hour before my alarm went off. Once my eyes opened, I was much too excited to go back to sleep, though I slept like a rock all night.

So, here I am at 5:15 A.M., making my morning coffee while dancing around the kitchen in my robe and house slippers. Dill is still on the bed, knocked out. I think he noticed I smelled like a new person last night, and he didn't seem to care for it.

I remember the promise I made to Joseph last night, that I wouldn't be up before dawn. The sun hasn't begun to rise yet, but I'm not going to call him until at least 7:00.

I've already packed my toaster, so instead of having a nice, warm piece of toast, I open a pack of PopTarts and take a bite off the corner before pushing all of the boxes stacked in the kitchen over to the door leading out to the garage.

I decide on carrying the smaller ones out to fill my car with, first. Then, I'll wedge some of the bigger ones into the trunk. Maybe that's backwards. I'm not a professional mover, obviously, but I'm beginning to regret not hiring one.

One by one, I haul the boxes to my little Camry. I remember the day I moved into this house. Little Camry bore that load, too. Today is a whole lot more special. And hopefully, it will be the last move for me.

Just as I'm shutting the trunk of my car, full of tightly taped and stacked boxes, I hear the sound of my phone's ringtone from the kitchen counter. I glance at my watch as I briskly head back through the opened garage door and into the kitchen. 6:45 A.M.

Could it be Jill? It's almost time for her to get off from work. If it was an easy morning, she may have some down-time right now. Truthfully I hope it's *not* Jill. Surprisingly, I haven't told her anything about Joseph and I. She doesn't even know he'd called me the other night, much less that we had a date. I guess you could say I've been keeping him a secret all to myself thus far.

When I grab my phone from the countertop, though, I see that it's not Jill. Instead, it's Joseph.

I quickly put the phone to my ear. "Hello?"

"Good morning, beautiful. You sound good and awake," he says with a gravelly voice.

My heart flutters at the sound of his voice as he calls me beautiful.

"Well, I've been up for a while," I confess.

"You were going to call me when you woke up, *remember*?" he playfully chides.

"I was not about to call you when I woke up, at 5 A.M. You have to work tonight."

"I'll be just fine. Believe me, between the coffee and the criminals, I don't think I'll have any trouble staying awake. It *is* the weekend." He chortles sleepily, though I can tell he is up and stirring around from the faint sounds of metal against china.

"Well, still. I would have felt terrible waking you up that early. I was going to let you sleep until at least 7," I reply, as I swirl my cold cup of coffee.

"So, are you ready for me to come over, or do you need some more time?" Joseph asks.

"Well, my car is jammed about as full as I could pack it, so I guess whenever you're ready, come on over and we'll load your truck and make trip number one." As I say the words aloud, I can hardly believe this day has finally come.

"Give me about twenty minutes, and I'll be there," he says.

We hang up and I suddenly realize I must do something about my appearance.

I place my phone and coffee cup on the counter and hurriedly head back down the hall and into the bedroom. Dill is still sound asleep across the bed, living his best life without any idea that his best life will soon be lived somewhere else. In a much better place.

I quickly change from my large sweatshirt and lounge pants into another sweatshirt, but with jeans and a bra. I take my messy blonde hair down from the shabby, slept-in ponytail and brush it before pulling it back up, neater and with a few wisps pulled out around my face.

"That's better," I mumble.

But still, I open my old, crusty makeup bag and take out the blush palette and a fluffy brush to apply the makeup with. Each cheek gets a generous swipe of the brush. And now, for the final touch: the nearly-petrified mascara. I've got to get down to the drug store the first chance I get.

By the time I've taken Dill out, given him his treat, and am headed to rinse my coffee cup, I hear Joseph's truck rumbling into the driveway. Dill hears it too. He jumps up with his front paws against the door, his tail fanning the floor, and happily peers out. It's a good thing I bought puppy Dill as a companion rather than a guard dog.

"Hey! Come in." I greet him at the door just as he approaches it.

"You do have her loaded down," he comments with a chuckle as he passes by my car and glances through the windows.

"I told you I would. I'm trying to get all moved in ASAP," I reply.

"Well, show me the boxes and I'll get my truck loaded down, too," Joseph says.

"Okay, but first there's someone who really wants to meet you," I say as I reach for the door that Dill is patiently standing behind.

"Hey, buddy!" Joseph greets Dill as he squats down and rubs his belly.

"*Aww. Look!* He already likes you. He never just rolls onto his back for a stranger to pet him!" I laugh in disbelief.

"Yeah, you know good people, don't you, buddy? Yes, you're a good boy," Joseph coos as he gives Dill much appreciated belly scratches.

"Oh, he will love you forever, now," I promise.

Dill followed Joseph and I every step we made as we moved my pile of packed boxes out to the truck, watching most curiously.

Once we had Joseph's truck as full as we could fill it, I kissed Dill and told him to take a nap until I got back. The house is almost bare at this point, but he does still have the bed to sleep on.

"Alright, you lead the way," Joseph says with a wink as he climbs into his truck.

As I sit in the driver's seat of my loaded-down sedan, I can't believe this moment is happening. Not only am I moving into the home of my dreams, but look who's helping me with the move. It's in my nature to question if this is too good to be true.

As I drive down the winding country road leading to the farmhouse, I find myself glancing in the rear-view mirror more than necessary. Of course, he's always back there, following closely.

I impulsively switch the radio off and relish the peacefulness that comes with both the quiet countryside and the overwhelmingly surreal drive.

As I finally make the turn into my new driveway and head toward the tall white beauty, I marvel once again at the old home in all her glory. I stopped by yesterday after I signed the closing paperwork, but I'm not sure I could ever grow tired of the view from the driveway.

I back the car right up to the front porch steps before jumping out and popping the trunk, Joseph pulling in beside me. I locate the house key among the others on my key ring and walk around the car to wait for Joseph to get out of his truck.

"This place is *nice!*" He says as he stands from the truck and looks around the yard. "I definitely see you here," he adds with a nod.

"Thanks," I reply. "I do really love it. It reminds me so much of my childhood home. When I came across it, I *knew* it had to be mine."

The possibility of someday returning there to see the old home place with Joseph flashes to mind. Before now, it's always been totally out of the question for me.

"Well, show me the inside," he says as he walks closer to me and the house.

We walk up the two steps and onto the creaky covered porch as I fumble for the key again. He stands behind me, holding the screen door with his back, and I can feel his warmth and gaze on me.

Finally, I unlock the deadbolt and shove the heavy wooden door open with a screech.

Inside, it's as perfect as it was yesterday, albeit bare. But I'll be fixing that right away. In the nakedness of the empty house, all of the details and lovely imperfections are easily visible. The chippy white painted bead board walls, the scuffs and ridges along the worn hardwoods beneath our feet.

"It has such character all by itself, doesn't it?" I ask, although I don't necessarily need an answer.

"That it *does,*" he agrees.. "I like an old farmhouse. Reminds me of grandpa's place, in a way," he says.

We wander across the creaky floors as I show him each room in the house, covering the downstairs portion before moving to the hall staircase that turns into an L-shape and leads to a coat closet and two bedrooms. I've already chosen mine, of course. Although they're very similar to one another, the one I chose for my own bedroom is facing the eastern side of the house, overlooking the spacious front yard, where the morning sun will pour in through the large paned windows.

I get giddy thinking that the first morning I wake up in this house will only be in a couple of days.

"Well, that was the grand tour," I say as we land back on the first floor and head toward the living and dining area where we started. "I guess we'd better start unloading boxes, though. We've sure got plenty."

"Oh it won't take too long, and we'll be heading back to get another load," Joseph says. "You've already done the hard part of packing everything."

"Yeah, I guess you're right," I agree. "Although it didn't seem like much of a chore. I was happy to get my things out of the old house and ready for this one. Plus, I've been minimizing, so I really don't have *that* many belongings."

Outside on the porch, a gentle breeze fans the fallen leaves across the yard, and I stand still for just a moment as it cools my face, sending a cheerful shiver down my spine.

"Let's just stack them in the living room, and I'll sort them out later." I step off the porch toward my car, Joseph following closely behind.

"You sure you don't want me to help you move your furniture today?" He asks, carrying two large boxes up the porch steps.

"Oh yeah," I assure him with a wave. "Jill and Todd are glad to help, and I've got plenty here to keep me busy for a while. You need to rest up for work tonight."

"Alright, whatever you want. But I really don't mind," he says.

"I know. And thank you," I reply, truly thankful.

The two of us make trip after short trip to and from the house, retrieving the many boxes I've packed into both our vehicles as tightly as I could.

"We've just about got this load licked," Joseph says as he takes the last one from the bed of his truck.

"Thank goodness," I sigh. "I still have a couple more in my car. You're fast!"

He chuckles a bit as he walks past me toward the house with the cardboard box. "No, your car just had more in it than my truck did."

Just as he's walking back down the steps toward me, something catches my eye.

"Joseph!" I point at the window behind him before covering my opened mouth with fright.

"What?!" He spins around lightning quick, but it's gone before he can see anything.

"I saw a figure… of a person." I gulp.

"Where?" He asks, wearing deep concern on his face.

"That window," I say, pointing to the window next to the front door. "I saw a person walk by, plain as day."

I feel the blood rushing to my head, as my heart begins to drum so loudly it's audible to me.

"Stay right there," he gently instructs as he holds his hand out toward me. Then he opens the screen door and enters the house. I stand against my car to steady myself from the weakness in my knees, and watch as he walks around in the house, boldly investigating.

I can see him through the window as he goes from the living room into the dining area, in the same direction I saw the other person go. I bite my lip with anticipation as the moments pass.

I crane my neck to see if I can catch a glimpse of anything inside. Just then, I see Joseph walking toward the hallway, in the direction of the stairs. It's strange he didn't seem to find anyone downstairs, because I was here the whole time, and I didn't see anyone going toward the stairs. My mind races in circles as I wait and watch.

Finally, I decide to grab my phone out of the car just in case there's a need for it. Glancing over my shoulder for one last look at the front windows, I momentarily turn away and quickly retrieve my phone from the console of my car.

And in the same moment that I turn my back to the house, I hear the slam of the screen door. I nearly jump out of my own skin as I quickly snap my head around in the direction of the house. I see no one, though.

"Joseph?" I call from the yard as I stand with my legs trembling.

Where *is* he? I'm sure he's okay, but I don't like this uneasy feeling that's come over me. Who is in my house? And why did that door just slam with no sign of anyone around?

I suppose the wind could have possibly picked up the screen door and slammed it shut while my back was turned. I don't recall having felt any strong gust of wind, but then again, I was in the car for that brief second. Suddenly, I feel extra thankful that Joseph is here with me. I can't imagine how scared I'd be if I were alone right now.

I pace back and forth along the distance of the front of the house and around to the north side of it, looking for any signs of anyone outside, or through the windows. As I come back to the very front of the house where our vehicles are parked, I suddenly see Joseph standing at the front window where I'd seen the person passing by.

I hold up my hands in a shrug. "Well?" I call. "See anything?"

He leaves the window and walks out onto the front porch, down the steps and toward me. I see that he doesn't look well.

"Joseph…?" I say. "Are you okay?"

He walks across the grass and stands in front of me, his face white.

"Did you see anyone out here?" He asks, his voice a bit shaky.

"No. I heard the screen door slam, but I didn't see anyone. What's the *matter?*" I ask impatiently.

"That's what I thought." He looks as though he's about to faint any second.

"Joseph, come here and sit down. You're looking very weak right now," I say as I coax him toward the driver's seat of my car. He slowly walks to the car before collapsing onto the seat, still looking at me.

"You're scaring me. Please tell me what's going on," I plead with him.

"Okay," he takes a couple of deep breaths and attempts to steady himself. "I don't want you to freak out, Blaire."

"*What?!*" I ask, growing desperate for an explanation.

"I searched the entire house. Nobody was in there. But, when I came back through the living room, I could see you out the window. You were walking from that way, looking through the windows as you walked back here." He points toward the corner of the house.

"And Blaire…There was a woman with you."

He looks at me with deep concern, obviously still frightened.

His words chill me to the bone. "There was a woman with me?" I ask, as if I didn't quite understand him.

He nods. "I swear. I'm not crazy. I know it probably seems like I am right now."

As the color slowly begins to return to Joseph's face, I imagine it fading from mine as I suddenly feel as though I might pass out.

"Okay, and what did she look like?" I ask, squatting down beside him so that I don't fall.

"Older, gray-haired lady. Kind of short. She had on a purple sweater, I think. And, she had her arm around you," he says, looking away from me as he picks his fingernails.

"Whoa. W*hat*?" I feel the need to steady my breath as my heart rate increases yet again, thumping in my ears.

"I didn't think you were aware of her presence," he says. "You just kept walking and looking around with a concerned look on your face, not acknowledging anyone else. And then you shrugged when you saw me at the window. By the time I got from the window to the door, she had vanished."

As he says this, my mind flashes back to him standing at the window looking out at me. Goosebumps cover my entire body and the hair on my arms stand on end as I think of that very moment — such a short time ago – and what he was seeing as he looked out at me, and apparently someone else.

"I definitely was not aware of this presence," I state calmly, my mouth dry.

I look around, unsure of what to say or do next. The energy has been drained from me, along with the excitement I was feeling just a few minutes prior.

Finally, I sigh heavily and look up at Joseph who's still sitting in the driver's seat of my car, dumbfounded.

"Well, now what?" I ask, as if he has a solution to all of this up his sleeve.

"I don't know what, Blaire. I don't hardly know my own name right now," he says.

"I think I've moved enough for today," I say dryly, as I look down and pluck at blades of grass. "I'll somehow work up the courage to continue moving tomorrow, and that should be the last of it, besides furniture."

As I say the words, I'm fully aware that there is no longer excitement to accompany them. All emotions seem to have bled from the association with this place. All of them, that is, except fear.

"That's your call," he says. "I'm here to help all day if you want to continue."

"I don't know. I'm like, totally wiped out now. Are you serious? I bought a haunted house?" I ask rhetorically as I angrily toss a lone pebble I found in the grass.

"I *loved* this place," I whisper sadly.

"I'm wiped out too," Joseph replies. "I've never seen anything like that in my life. Never really believed in such, to be honest."

"I suppose you do, now." I look up to see him still wide-eyed, but he cracks the slightest hint of a smile in response to my comment.

"Yeah." he chuckles nervously. "I guess you could say that."

"Well, come with me to turn the lights out and lock the door," I say, standing up and dusting my pants off.

"Yes, ma'am," he replies as he follows me up the steps and across the creaky, wood porch.

I reach inside the door and quickly flip the light switch before slamming the door shut and turning the key.

"Okay, let's get out of here. I need to go lay down."

"I know what you mean," Joseph agrees. "I might just do the same after coming down from this adrenaline rush, but I doubt I'll be able to sleep."

"I feel so bad that this has happened," I tell him, genuinely. "I'm really sorry."

"Why are you sorry?" he asks, stunned. "You couldn't help it. You're just as shaken as I am, if not worse."

"Yeah, but you were just over here trying to help me, and I really appreciate it. You didn't know you were signing up to get scared half to death," I say.

"It's *alright*," he assures me and takes me in his arms as we stand on the front lawn between the two vehicles.

I look up at him as my heart begins to flutter again. This time, as the result of Joseph's warm body against mine. The fear, though still present, is being covered by the soft weight of comfort that he's effortlessly providing.

I lay my head on his chest and melt into his arms as I stare through the large dark window into the house. I know that soon I will feel dread at the thought of spending the night alone in the house, but right now the feeling is snuffed down beneath the surface, drowned out by the happiness that comes from being held by the man I've always longed for.

I'm not sure how long we stood together in the front yard; it could have been seconds or hours. But eventually, the embrace is reluctantly broken and following it is his promise to call me tonight on his way to work.

We part ways at the end of the gravel drive, Joseph turning left to travel deeper into the country and myself right, towards Weatherford.

The drive home is a blur. I don't remember getting here, but suddenly I'm sitting in the car in the silence of the garage, my face wet with tears.

Through the window of the door, I can see Dill's face and front paws as he patiently waits for me to come inside. I look at myself in the rearview mirror and discover that my eyes are bloodshot and black streams of mascara run down my face.

Before heading in, I check the time to see that it's only noon. I have no appetite for lunch, whatsoever. All I really want to do is lay across the bed and wake to find that today was just a nightmare. Maybe it's still the night before, Joseph and I have had a great time at the fair and I'm sleeping soundly while dreaming of the following day.

I know that's not the case. I couldn't dream this up, even if I were experiencing side effects of a newly developed medication.

"Hey, buddy," I greet Dill as I reach for his leash by the door. "Let's go out."

Dill can sense my shift in mood. He follows me around the mostly empty house, poking me with his cold nose.

"It's okay, Dill. You're a good boy," I tell him as I briefly pet his ears.

I grab my phone from my bag and then I fall onto the couch. "Come on," I call to Dill as I pat the cushion. He jumps onto the couch with me and lays down on the opposite end, though he's so big we're still touching. I run my fingers through his soft curly coat as I lay still and reflect on the day.

How did things go so wrong, so quickly? Just this morning, I was absolutely euphoric, and a few hours later, I feel as though I have weights tied to all of my limbs. Like all of the excitement and joy the new house brought me has been unfairly stolen.

My eyes burn from the cry I apparently had on the car ride home, and suddenly I can't seem to hold them open. I feel myself drifting further into a much-needed slumber.

FOURTEEN
ISAIAH 43:1-2

The next thing I know, the sound of my phone ringing is waking me from a deep sleep. I fumble around on the couch, feeling for the phone while Dill whines for me to stop the noise.

My hand finally lands on the phone, and I turn it around to see that it's Jill calling. I suddenly realize she is calling me while on her way to work. I've slept on the couch for five hours. I swipe the screen.

"Hello?" I answer, sleepily.

"Were you *asleep*?" She asks. "I figured you'd be moving into your new house."

Her words should bring me joy, but hearing them brings a sucker punch to my gut instead.

"Yeah, see we have some catching up to do. There's a lot I haven't told you about the last couple of days," I explain as I sit upright on the couch beside Dill.

"Oh?" She asks, perplexed. "What have I missed?"

"I guess I'll just start at the beginning. So, you know Joseph… the cute guy that visits Mrs. Simms, right?” I don't wait for her answer. She knows who Joseph is.

“Um, we had a date last night…” it almost sounds like a question.

“What? And you didn't tell me? Where? How did it go?” She asks all of the questions at once.

“Well, it went great…” This part of the story does make me smile.

“We went to the fair, and we had a really good time,” I say, remembering last night which now seems like so long ago.

“Ooh, the fair,” Jill comments. I can't tell if she's being sarcastic or serious, but I continue.

“He's so sweet. He volunteered to come help me move today.”

“And did he?” Jill asks, rather impatiently.

“He did,” I reply. “He came over early and we filled his truck. Then he followed me over, and we unloaded my car and his truck into the farmhouse.”

“Did you get it all in one trip?” Jill questions a bit suspiciously.

“Well, no. See, this is where things sort of take a turn,” I explain.

“Oh, no. Blaire, he had better hope he didn't do anything to hurt you. I swear —”

“No, Jill. Nothing like that,” I assure her. “He's great. Like, really great.”

“Okay.” She sighs a breath of relief.

“But, while we were moving, we both saw something….*supernatural.*” Speaking the words makes chills return to every inch of my skin.

“*What?*” Jill is intrigued. “Well, what happened? What did you see?”

"Well," I begin. "We were in the yard, all alone, and I saw...*very clearly*... the figure of a person standing in the front window. Joseph goes right in to check it out. He doesn't see *anyone* in the entire house. Until he comes back to the front window and looks out," I pause.

"And? What did he see?" Jill prods anxiously.

"An old woman...with her arm around me."

"Shut up!" Jill exclaims. "And you didn't see her?"

"Nope. I was just in the yard freaking out a little bit because I'd seen someone in my house and then I heard the screen door slam, but no one was there...and then Joseph had yet to return even though I'd called his name," I recall the chilling events of this morning.

"Wait, you saw the person...or whatever... inside the house. Then the screen door opens and shuts all by itself...and then the woman is seen outside with her arm around you." Jill confirms this as more of a statement than a question.

"Yep, that's pretty much what happened," I say, still rattled at the memory of it.

"Oh, my gosh," Jill says. "That's like something out of a movie or something. That's really wild."

"Yeah, it's pretty much ruined my excitement about the house, if I'm being honest," I admit, resting my pounding head in the palm of my hand.

"Have you asked your real estate agent anything about it?" Jill asks. "Maybe he knows something that he'd be willing to disclose... you know, now that you've signed the paperwork..." she chuckles.

"No. What good will that do? He doesn't know anything. Besides, I'd be too embarrassed."

"You're probably right. Well, if you wanted to, you could do some research on the house yourself. Find out about the history of the home. That might make it less scary somehow," Jill says.

"No, that would not make it less scary," I argue. "Suppose I find out something totally horrifying. I'm already dreading the first night alone in the house at this point."

"This stinks," Jill says empathetically. "You've been so excited. You love that house so much; this doesn't hardly seem fair."

"I know," I agree. "The whole script has *flipped* on me."

"So, what now? Are you moving more tomorrow?" she asks.

"I suppose." I sigh.

Suddenly, the beep of an incoming call interrupts my depressing thoughts. I take the phone from my ear and check it.

"That's Joseph calling," I say. "He's probably on his way into work, too."

"Yeah, I just pulled in at The Home," Jill says. "I'll call you later."

We end our call, and I answer Joseph's. His voice is a retreat from the lonely cycle of self-pity and anxiety I've been stuck in.

"What have you been up to?" he asks.

"Well, I came home and collapsed onto the couch where I knocked out for five solid hours," I admit.

"Good," he says. "You must've needed that. I took a good nap myself."

"Oh, I'm glad. How're you feeling?" I ask.

"Good as new," he replies. "How are you holding up?"

"Good as new? That must've been *some* nap," I comment with a chuckle.

"I'm not going to let what happened today get me down," he says. "Yes, it shook me up a bit, but I'm fine now. Really."

"Well, I envy you for your resilience," I reply. "I mean, don't get me wrong. I'm glad you're doing well and that it hasn't affected you mentally or anything like that. I'm just still pretty shaken up, I'm worried about staying there alone, and I'm honestly sulking at the fact that the happiest event that has happened to me since I can remember, has been stolen from me."

"I know how you must feel," he says. "But try to keep your chin up. I've heard that if you ignore these types of spirits and things, they won't bother you at all."

"You're such a comfort." I giggle.

"Well, I'm trying," he says.

"You actually *are* a comfort. More than you even know," I tell him. "If it weren't for you, I don't know what state of mind I'd be in. Can you imagine if I'd been there alone today during all of that?"

"Well, how about this," he begins to suggest. "How about we put this behind us, try to forget about it, and look forward to what's to come? And I'll be there to help move, or whatever you need, first thing Monday morning, I promise."

That *is* a nice thought. Anything that involves Joseph is a nice thought. Maybe he's right. Everything will be okay, won't it??

"You're probably right," I agree. "You know, I remember not too long ago, I told someone that I loved the house so much, nothing could take away the happiness I have because of it."

"I seem to have forgotten that," I think aloud.

"That's my girl," he says. "I knew you were tougher than that." My heart clenches in my chest at the sound of him calling me his girl.

"You know, I think you're the only one who I've ever let by with that," I say with a smile.

"By with what?" he asks.

"Calling me *your* girl."

"Oh! I see." he chuckles, seemingly embarrassed.

"It's okay. I'll be your girl if you want me to."

That last part slipped out before I could stop it. I feel like a fool. What are you, Blaire, a high school girl? My goodness.

"Oh, really? Well, alright, if you insist. It's settled, then."

I grin to myself, so broad that I think my face may split.

"Oh, by the way…" he changes the subject, but my smile doesn't fade.

"About Addie. I've searched high and low, and I just can't find anything at all. I thought I'd get some sort of lead, but I've got nothing. I'm sorry," he says.

"*Addie!*" I exclaim. "I think that's *exactly* what I need!" The sudden revelation excites me as I recall the comfort I find in the words of Addie's diary.

"Why didn't I think of her sooner?" I ask, more to myself than Joseph.

"You've been in sort of a brain fog," he reminds me. "Plus, you did say you wanted to save the rest of the diary to read on the lonely nights in the new house. Don't forget *that,"* he says, careful not to mention that there's now increased necessity.

"I did say that," I agree. "But if ever I needed some comfort, I'd say today is the day. Besides, you know what's going to happen?" I ask.

"What's that?"

"I'm going to get to the end of the diary, and there it will be: Her full name and street address, somewhere in the final entry. Then, I can just call her and invite her over. See? Wouldn't that be amazing?"

"I like your theory. I hope it works out for you," he says with a snicker and just a touch of sarcasm.

"Thanks," I say. "And thanks for the awesome reminder, although I'm honestly baffled that I needed one."

I continue, "It's just so amazing, really. Every mental or emotional hardship I've encountered seems to mirror Addie's in some way. Though she has a much different outlook than I've had."

"Oh really?" he asks. "How's that?"

"Well," I begin. "She endured great loss when her son died. And then she lost her husband. She seems to really have no one, except her best friend… and her patients."

"I just read about her retiring, which is super difficult for her, mentally. She needs knee surgery and that also has her worried. But I'll bet she's one of the most pleasant people to be around. You'd just have to read her words I guess, to understand what I mean. Her thoughts she's written down reflect her inward emotions, fears and all. But I get the feeling she's a very strong woman, outwardly."

"Hmm. Kind of like someone else I know," Joseph hints. "I can understand why you like reading this diary so much. You never really know what people are feeling just by passing them by, or even talking with them, I guess."

"Yeah, you're right," I agree. "I'm so glad I have this. It's really helped me cope with my own feelings and how I view life in a lot of ways.."

"Yeah, I'll bet. That's pretty neat," he says. "I'm sure your outlook on life has always been just fine though, and you certainly are a pleasant person to be around. There's another thing you might have in common with this Addie."

"Well, thanks. You see positive things in me that aren't even there. No wonder I like you," I say.

He stifles a laugh. "So, what're your plans for the rest of the night?" he asks, shifting our conversation into a more lighthearted one.

"Well, I'm thinking about ordering a pizza for delivery and then cuddling up on the couch with Addie's diary. So exciting, huh?"

"Sounds like fun," he says. "If I weren't at work, I'd love to come by and hang out with you. Not to have an Addie's diary reading, but to maybe watch a movie or something." He chuckles softly.

"Yeah, that also sounds like fun. I hate you're working. You're off after tomorrow night, right?" I ask.

"Yes, ma'am. Tonight and tomorrow night, and then I have a few off. You'll want some help unpacking, or you'd rather do that yourself?" he asks.

"Oh yeah, I'd be glad for you to help!" I say, though I'd just be glad to have his company, truthfully.

"Well, I guess I've got to go for now. I'm on the clock," he says. "I'll text you in a little while, okay?"

"Okay. Be careful," I say, realizing for the first time how devastated I'd be if something were to happen to him.

We end our call, and I immediately call for the delivery of a medium pepperoni, olives, and mushroom topped pizza with extra butter for dipping and a large brownie. I'm so hungry that just about anything sounds good right now. I hope the driver doesn't take forever.

"Dill!" I call, waking him from his warm spot on the couch. "Need to go potty?" He rouses and stretches his long legs, yawning, before jumping off the couch and sauntering slowly to the kitchen.

"Come on," I say as I bend down to clip the leach onto his collar.

We stay out a while longer this time. I want to let him get as much exercise and fresh air as possible while I'm home with him these next couple of weeks. But we don't stay too long because down the street and through some neighbor's trees, I see a car with a glowing Pizza Hut sign on the top of it, coming around a curve toward my house.

Inside, I grab my purse off the kitchen table and quickly dig my wallet from the bottom of it while Dill loudly laps up water from his dish.

After paying the pizza delivery guy, I dart straight down the hall and into the bedroom where I pick up the diary from the bedside table. It feels like years since I've opened it, though it's really only been a few days. A few *eventful* days.

Taking the whole box of pizza, a cold *La Croix,* and Addie's diary, I make myself comfortable on the couch once again. Dill is busy in the kitchen with his peanut butter-filled Kong toy or he'd certainly have his giant head inside my pizza box.

I open the diary and flip to the last place I left off, recalling Addie's feelings of bittersweetness as she attended her last birth and the dread of her upcoming surgery. Suddenly, I'm giddy with eagerness to step back into the realm of Addie. Wherever she may be in the world, somehow her words on paper invite me to experience a taste of her life and remind me that I'm not the only person who endures emotional challenges, and that life does go on, with ebbs and flows of the good and bad.

FIFTEEN
PROVERBS 31:30

*T*he pain is severe. Both in my post-operative knee and the reflection I see when I look upon the days past. I should rejoice at a life well-lived, rather than mourning, but I'm finding that to be difficult.

I feel strongly that I'm nearing the end of my time on Earth. I cannot explain the reason for my prediction. There's nothing in my chart to indicate that my time is approaching anytime soon. There's no chronic disease or terminal illness looming over me, ready to snatch me from this world.

Most people, when faced with the question of: "what would be the ideal way to go?" might say 'quickly' or maybe to 'just fall asleep'. I would have to agree that either of those would be the preferred choice over the gloom of impending death that many older or chronically ill people must face.

I hardly ever leave my room here in the rehabilitation unit except to go down to the gym when the therapists come for me, but I see the demented and helpless invalids being carted up and down the hall... to the dining area, or to the living room to watch a movie. Many of them stay asleep all day, chronic pain likely the only thing keeping them aware of their own existence.

I can find some comfort in the fact that I'm not likely to ever be in that sad state of being. I don't believe I'll last long enough to see the end of life dragging on and on in that way, with the bittersweet end hovering just out of reach. What a peaceful relief it will be for many of these folks in this place. Myself included.

My knee operation went fairly well. Uneventful, anyway. The recovery portion has been less than satisfactory, but much of that has to do with the mental hurdles that I refuse to jump. I skipped right over the denial and the anger, and I'm now hovering somewhere between the depression and acceptance phase of the death and dying emotional roadblocks.

The therapists and nurses here are unaware that my hourglass is nearly empty. If they thought for one second that my mind was in this place, they'd have me signed up to see the psychiatrist quicker than I could wink my eye. Before the end of the week, I'd be being fed some sort of antidepressant and be participating in routine mental assessments.

But me, I'd prefer to get this knee healed up as quickly as possible so that I can get home where I'll draw my final breath. We don't need any set-backs or additional dramatic interventions to add to my plan of care. So, I've been most cooperative during my stay here. I go to therapy when they come for me, I let the nurse strap the robotic monstrosity onto my leg three times every day while patiently enduring the pain that it causes. Because I am not fond of the way those narcotic drugs make me feel, I only ask for two Tylenol tablets before undergoing the machine therapy that works my leg back and forth. Afterwards, I apply to it an arnica gel that I brought from home, which makes the pain manageable enough to sleep through until someone wakes me again.

Madge has been wonderful company on the long and dreariest of days. She comes by and brings me my mail, late-blooming flowers from my garden, or a stack of puzzle books. She's kept me in decent food, as well. There's no way a body can heal on the processed meals they serve here. Madge has been so kind to keep me a thermos full of herbal tea at my bedside, sliced bread that I made ahead and stored in the freezer, and boiled eggs from my laying hens.

I could never ask for a truer friend than Madge. She acts as if she isn't one bit tired, but I know better. Perhaps I can persuade her to come and stay with me at my home when I am discharged from here. Then, we could look after each other for the time that I have remaining.

As of late, many fond memories of my dear beloved Michael have resurfaced quite often. Thoughts of the first time I looked at his beautiful face, and then the last, as he waved goodbye from the window seat of that military bus. Both were days filled with overwhelming emotion, from pure joy to immense sorrow. Many other emotions filled my days as a result of being Michael's mother, mostly happiness and pride.

My beloved Isaiah's presence has surely been with me through the throws of emotional and physical pain

I've endured since the operation. I've felt him here alongside me more than I ever have since his departure, so long ago. It's as if he's pushing me along, whispering "You've got to be strong, darling. You've got to get out of here and get home." And "home", I perceive to mean my Heavenly home, beyond the physical one. It is imperative for me to get to the home of comforting familiarity before advancing to the one of Heavenly wonders, where magnificent beauty and immeasurable peace are eternally abundant.

The staff here are mostly pleasant and diligent. I can tell that this facility is sorely understaffed, which creates problems for everyone involved. Luckily, I don't ask for much - just the necessities, like a handholding over to the commode when needed. The young volunteers stop in at least once per day and invite me down to play Bingo or to work a puzzle with the others who are attempting to recover from surgeries or near death experiences as the result of old age. I always respectfully decline their invitation.

There is one nurse, in particular, in which I am very fond of. She is, of course, always busy just like the rest of them. Maybe even more so, but she finds true joy in caring for her patients. I can see the spark of eagerness to help not only me, but others as well, as she kneels in the hallway beside an invalid in a wheelchair to talk softly to them as if she's got all the time in the world. However, I can see past that spark in her eyes, to the bitter-cold loneliness behind it. Though she tries, she can't hide from me the sadness that lingers deep within her sea-blue eyes.

From the bits of conversations we've had, I've gathered that she's unmarried. The love of her life is her poodle and the years-old memories she clings so tightly to, though I gathered the latter on my own.

Blaire. I have her name etched into my memory for when it comes time to brag on "star employees" the day I check out of here.

I'm weary, so I think I should set my pen aside and rest until Madge arrives with my supper, or an aide knocks to ensure that I'm still breathing.

I cannot be certain when I will again feel like writing. For now, I must grip the plow tightly with both weary hands. I must satisfy the powers that be over the Sunny Meadows nursing home so that I can return to my familiar haven before my time is up.

-Addie

SIXTEEN
JAMES 4:7-8

My hands are shaking as I hold the opened diary before me, staring down in unbelief at the words I've just read.

"Ms. Adelaide," I say aloud. "Addie is Ms. Adelaide Fisher."

How can this be, I wonder.

We took care of Ms. Adelaide a couple of years ago at The Home, I recall, as I easily visualize her face.

I close my eyes and pull from the depths of my memories, straining my bewildered mind to recall her story. Where did she go from Sunny Meadows? Did she complete her therapy? Was she re-admitted to the hospital? For the life of me, I can't remember.

I do remember being fond of Ms. Adelaide. She was pleasant and so quiet you'd barely know she was there. I can remember her homemade meals and natural creams she was allowed to keep at bedside. Her long gray hair was kept brushed and swept to the side, unless she was leaving the room for therapy, in which case she would pin it up into a neat little ball.

Beyond that, I don't remember things like the details of our conversations or any specifics regarding her care.

I wish I could go back and tell myself to spend every free moment at Addie's bedside, soaking up her wisdom and sharing deep and meaningful conversations with her, while we took the edge off each other's stinging loneliness. It saddens me to tears to realize how special and how troubled she was. And I had no idea. I only had the time enough to administer her medications, place the CPM machine on her leg, and sprint on to the next patient. How sad she must've been.

"You're so *stupid,* Blaire," I say as I swipe a tear from my cheek.

Standing from the couch, I rush to the kitchen carrying the diary and the box full of pizza, still untouched. I glance at the clock and see that it's almost 9:00 PM. Jill will be finishing up the nighttime medication round soon.

I shove my feet into my brown clogs by the door and grab my phone and keys from the countertop. "I'll be back, Dill," I promise. Then, leaving the kitchen light on for him, I rush out the door and shuffle to the car, tossing Addie's diary onto the passenger seat as I slide in behind the wheel.

I travel the familiar route to The Home, inconsiderate of the speed limit as I go full force ahead. My mind and heart race in unison as I not only try to recall more details about Addie, but also attempt to fathom that I've *met* her. I've talked to and cared for the lady whom I've grown to love through her lost diary.

"I've just got to find her. I'm so close now," I say to myself in the pitch-black car as I speed through a yellow traffic light.

Two more turns, and I'm racing up the curved drive toward my destination. The familiar brick building somehow looks different tonight. More inviting than usual, perhaps.

I nearly run across the parking lot and up the wooden stairs to the landing, where I punch the code into the keypad and fling the door open. The nurses' station is empty; Jill must still be passing out bedtime medications. I march briskly through the small room, around the corner and down the hallway in the direction of Jill's parked medicine cart.

I quietly dart in and out of the rooms of sleeping residents as I try to locate Jill. She has to be close, but where is she?

"Jill?" I call, maybe a bit too frantically.

Jill comes running out of the very last room on the wing. "Blaire?" She looks at me, visibly concerned. "What are you doing here?" she asks.

"I need the key to medical records," I spurt out without an explanation.

"Why?" she asks. "Is everything okay?"

"Yes, and no," I swipe my clammy forehead.

"Did you see another ghost?" she asks as she fumbles for the key to the medical records door.

"What? No, I'd temporarily forgotten all about that, actually. Wait until you get a load of *this*," I say, short of breath as I hold the diary up for her to see.

Jill's eyes widen. "What *is* it?" she asks, intrigued.

"Just follow me," I answer. "I'll tell you everything."

Inside the small closet that contains thousands of manilla folder-filled documents on the last who-knows-how-many years' worth of patients, I take a deep breath and sit down on the carpeted floor.

"Okay," I begin as Jill takes a seat next to me.

"Do you remember Adelaide Fisher?" I ask.

"Yeah," Jill answers. "Real sweet little lady in room 107. Total knee, I think. Why?"

I swallow hard as I hold the diary up. *"Because she's Addie,"* I say, still in disbelief.

"What?" Jill asks, shocked. "You've got to be kidding me. Are you sure?"

"Yes, I'm sure. She even mentions me here in her diary."

I look down at the book in my hands, my eyes burning.

"I didn't even know her nickname was Addie," I whisper before surrendering to the weight of the tears that fill my eyes and fall onto my lap. I rest my head in my hands, and there on the floor by Jill, I weep.

"Oh, Blaire…It's okay," she says as she wraps her arms around my shoulders and rests her head against mine. "You had no idea."

I had no idea, but that's the whole problem. How could I care for someone every day and miss so many things about them?

When I gain my composure a bit, I stand up and wipe my eyes.

"Okay," I begin, sniffling, as I tuck a loose strand of hair behind my ear. "We have to find her chart. You go ahead if you need to finish up the med pass or anything, but I'll be in here."

"No, I'm good for a while," Jill says. "I just finished medicating Mr. Horace. I saved the best for last." She giggles as she rolls her eyes.

"Do you know what kind of order they keep these files in?" I ask, running my finger along the first row.

"Yeah, I had to come in here late one evening and pull an old chart for the state surveyors once," Jill answers as she walks to the back shelf of the tiny dimly lit room.

"So, I think it goes chronologically by last name, and each rack is a different time frame. She was here, what, two years ago maybe?" Jill asks, reaching up and thumbing through the files on the top shelf.

"If my memory serves me," I reply.

"She's probably here on this rack," she points to the second one from the door and we both kneel and begin our search for the "F" section.

"Okay," Jill finally says. "Here's Albert Flannigan. You remember him?"

"I think so," I reply as I weakly try to recall.

"Addie must be in this general area," I say as I begin taking out handfuls of "F" folders.

"Fagan, Felder, Finch...*Fisher, Adelaide*. I've got it!" I exclaim, pulling the folder from the stack.

I sit back with my legs folded beneath me and quickly open the cover of Ms. Adelaide's chart. Jill crawls over and sits next to me, peering over at the chart with anticipation.

There, fixed to the inner cover of the folder with a paperclip, is a picture of Addie sitting in a wheelchair on the day she was admitted to Sunny Meadows. I take the picture and look closely at it. Though she looks tired, with dark half-circles beneath her eyes and a gentle smile forced through pain, I see beauty. I see *Addie,* the midwife, mother, widow, farmer, healer, influencer. Taking a deep, shaky breath, I open the cover of her diary and place the picture inside it before closing it again.

"Adelaide M. Fisher 04/15/1942," I read aloud.

I trace my finger along the face sheet, skimming the allergy section and the very short list of diagnoses. Past the primary care physician's information and Addie's admission weight, I stop at the contact list.

"Here it's got Madge MacGreggor as the only contact," I say as I hold my finger in the spot on the page. I reach into my pocket for my phone and snap a picture of Madge's number, just in case I should need it.

"Whatcha doing?" Jill asks.

"I might need her number, you never know," I explain with a shrug.

"Do you remember Madge?" Jill asks.

"Yes, but vaguely," I reply. "I saw a flash of her when she'd come in and out. I can't quite picture much more than a general description of her. She was tall, with white bobbed hair, if I remember correctly. She definitely wasn't a needy visitor; I always kind of got the feeling she wished to avoid staff for some reason. Like the kind who sneak in things that the patients aren't supposed to have. You know the kind."

Jill chuckles. "I do know. Like Mr. Tate's daughter with the tobacco and pocket knives. Remember that?"

Jill continues without waiting for my answer. "Madge must've always left before my shift began. I don't think I ever got to meet her."

"Well, I might have to contact her, if I can't locate Addie. But first, I'm going to see what else I can find out from the chart," I say, turning my attention back to the stack of papers on my lap.

Turning the page to the back side of the face sheet, I locate the information I came here in search of.

Personal information:

Address - 909 Craggy Pine Road. Bascomb, NC

My eyes widen as I hold the folder closer. Once again, my stomach lurches and seems to collide with my rapidly beating heart.

"Oh, my God!" I throw my head back, my eyes meeting the tiled ceiling. Chill bumps cover my arms as I draw a ragged breath.

"I don't believe this," I cry out, as tears begin to pour again from my stinging red eyes.

"What *is* it??" asks Jill, looking curiously from me to the chart in my hands, and back at me.

"Look at her home address," I say, expressionless, as I stare blankly at the words printed on the paper.

"Sounds familiar," Jill says after glancing at the documents in my shaky hands.

I look directly in Jill's eyes and remind her in a quiet and shaky voice,

"That's my new address."

Jill becomes speechless and we sit in silence for a moment as I attempt to gather the thoughts that swirl around like a tornado inside my head, leaving me stunned and sorting through the wreckage.

Suddenly, I begin to laugh, unable to help myself. "What are the odds? I mean... how does this even happen?"

Jill just shakes her head in disbelief, eyes still wide. "Wow," is all she can utter.

I don't even know what to think at this point," I admit. "My brain feels kind of numb after all of this."

"This is so crazy," comments Jill.

I don't think crazy accurately describes the day's events. Perhaps there's not a sufficient word.

"What are you going to do, now?" Jill asks.

Suddenly, as if I've been shocked, I jump at the diary lying on the floor beside me.

Jill watches intently as I flip to the last page I read. I flip beyond that page. Blank. I continue to flip the pages, one by one. Blank, blank, blank.

"That's it," I whisper. "This was the last thing she wrote." I pass the diary slowly to Jill.

As she reads the words Addie wrote during her stay here at our workplace, the rollercoaster continues as adrenaline fades and a bit of sadness creeps back in.

At some point, Jill has left me alone, though I'm not sure when, or what beckoned her retreat. Perhaps a patient yelled for help. Perhaps the fire alarm sounded. Maybe one of the aides saw the keys in the doorknob and came in, looking for Jill. Whatever it was, I daydreamt through it.

I've found myself still folded up on the floor of the medical records closet alone, my knees stiff and feet tingly. I'm not sure how much time has elapsed since I began reading through Addie's chart.

I carefully read each word, clinging to the last bit of Addie's life that I seem to have left. I read my own nurse's notes I'd written when I cared for her, seemingly ages ago. All of the notes indicate that she was a pleasant, compliant patient in the eyes of every nurse that cared for her.

The very last note was written by Carrie, the nurse that cares for my set of patients opposite my schedule. She'd written Addie's discharge note, stating that she had left the facility for home via friend Madge MacGreggor's personal vehicle and the in-house physical therapist had written an order for a Home Health agency to follow up.

I rub my burning eyes with my fingertips before attempting to stretch my legs out from underneath me. As I slowly stand and stretch my legs, I hear the slamming of the dining room door. That must be the dietary staff coming in to begin preparing breakfast. How long have I been sitting here?

I check my watch to see that I've been investigating Addie's files for hours. It's nearly 5 o' clock in the morning.

Placing the chart carefully back on the shelf where it was found, I pick the diary up from the floor and crack the door, peering down the hall into the empty dining room. Looking to the left, I see that Jill has pushed her medicine cart midway down the hall. She must be passing out Synthroid tablets and checking fasting blood sugar levels.

I dash down the hall toward the cart, being careful not to be seen. I don't want to have to explain myself if someone sees me here at the crack of dawn wearing sweats. Jill exits the room of Mrs. Simms.

"Hey," she says. "Did you get your research done? I was about to come check on you again."

The "again" suggests that she came in to check on me sometime, without my noticing.

"Yeah, I read every word of that old chart," I reply. "I think I'm going to call Joseph. He tried to text me a couple of times last night and I didn't even realize it. I'm going to see if he wants to meet me for breakfast when he gets off work. And after that, I'm going to try and reach Madge. Maybe she can verify things one way or the other."

"Blaire, what you *need* to do is go home and get some sleep. You're absolutely worn out," she says in the kindest way possible.

I *am* absolutely worn out. "I'm okay," I say. "I took a long nap yesterday."

"Well, please be careful driving," she says. "I can tell you're mentally exhausted."

After saying goodbye to Jill, I scurry down the hall and through the nurses' station to the exit door before anyone catches a glimpse of me. The spiral stairs leading down to the parking area look intimidating as I stand in the darkness on the landing, my frazzled stupor impairing my balance.

One by one, I slowly make it down the stairs, clinging to the wooden handrail with each step. Once in the car, I search my recent call log for Joseph's number.

It only rings once. "Hello?" he answers.

"Hey," I reply. "You busy?"

"No, it's been a slow night. Is everything okay? You're up early."

"Yeah, I've been up all night. Luckily, I had that nap yesterday," I remind him.

"What's the matter?" he asks. "Why have you been up all night?"

"It's a really long story," I say, pressing on the bridge of my nose as the pressure temporarily relieves the tension across my forehead.

"Could you meet me at Lucille's Restaurant when you get off?" I ask. The small country diner is just down the road from The Home.

"Sure, I can. I will be getting off in just a few minutes. But, what's the matter? You're worrying me."

"I just have something to show you," I answer. "Something I found. And I could *really* use some coffee and a giant plate of food."

I could also really use a few minutes in the company of Joseph.

"Okay, I can meet you in about thirty minutes," he says.

I'm sure to fall asleep if I sit in my car for any length of time waiting for him, so I decide to drive around with my window down, taking the longest way to Lucille's. The cool early morning air blows my hair about my face and sends shivers down my spine.

Daylight begins to break, revealing the dark, hazy mountain line in the distance. I turn into the parking lot of Lucille's Restaurant, which is already beginning to fill up with old pickup trucks and Buicks. Joseph has beat me here, I can see as I pull into a space beside his patrol car. He's standing beside the car, waiting for me in his slick black uniform.

I glance at myself in the rear-view mirror and see a ghoulish face looking back at me. What's left of yesterday's makeup is streaked over the darkened skin beneath my bloodshot eyes. My disheveled ponytail has fallen into a loose mess, wisps falling around my pale face.

I grab my wallet from the console before reaching into the passenger seat for the diary.

Outside, the smell of bacon surrounds the little cottage-like building.

"Please excuse my appearance," I say as I approach Joseph, wearing the same clothes I wore yesterday.

"You look tired, but still beautiful," he says with a smile as he places his hand in the middle of my back and walks me to the door of the bustling restaurant.

"I don't feel beautiful," I say with a forced chuckle as we step into the warmth of the small dimly lit diner.

"It's been forever since I've eaten here," I comment. We walk past the small section that's separated from the dining area with white lattice. I notice that it hasn't changed at all since the last time I was here. Illuminated with only a lamp, the entrance is still filled with locally sourced handmade things for sale, such as jellies, jams, and crocheted dish cloths.

We find a small empty table among the many others filled with older men conversing over cups of steamy black coffee.

Before we have sat completely in our seats, the burly, pleasant waitress named Angie is already asking for our orders. We both glance at the menu before spurting off our requests, as she nods and turns toward the kitchen, without ever even taking the ink pen from behind her ear.

"I think I'd better get some food in me before I tell you what I've discovered," I say, placing my hand on Addie's diary which is lying on the table next to the piping hot coffee that Angie has already brought over. "I'm like… depleted of everything."

"I take it, it has something to do with Addie?" Joseph guesses.

"Mm-hmm," I nod, gazing sleepily into his eyes.

"You seem strangely calm," he says.

"Well, I've simmered down quite a bit over the last couple of hours. I think I'm entering survival mode." I snicker weakly.

"You're probably right," Joseph nods.

"This place is always speedy," he says, glancing around the dining room. "You should be able to eat soon."

Within seconds of Joseph's prediction, Angie is, indeed, standing by our table with two large, smoking breakfast platters.

"Wow that *was* fast," I comment as Angie places my plate of sausage, eggs, and grits in front of me.

"Oh, this smells *so* good," I say as I pick up the fork from the table. "I'm used to skipping meals when it's busy at work, but I haven't eaten in a *really* long time. And even then, it was a Pop-Tart, of all things."

"Well, I hope you eat every bite," Joseph says as he samples a piece of bacon from his own plate.

Between delicious bites of breakfast food, I try to make small talk, but my mind is on Addie.

"Okay," I begin once my body is satisfied enough to allow me to turn some of my attention to the matter at hand.

I open the diary, leaving it lying on the table between Joseph and I, Addie's picture serving as a place holder of the last entry she made.

Joseph glances at the diary on the table while buttering a hot biscuit. Suddenly, he stops and points at the picture using his butter knife.

"Hold on a minute," he says, a look of utter perplexity on his face. "Can I see that picture?"

I pick it up and hand it to him, as his facial expression grows into a look of bewilderment.

He looks closely at the picture. "Well, I'll be," he finally utters as if he belongs at the table full of grandpas next to us.

"Do you know that woman?" I ask.

"I can't say I know her, but that's the woman I saw through the window at your new house," he answers with certainty.

I'm silent for a long moment, before finally replying, "I thought so." I feel as though a heavy weight has been lifted from me as I receive the confirmation of what I've suspected since late last night.

"Look, she's even wearing the same purple sweater in the picture," he points out matter-of-factly, again using his knife.

I take the picture from his hand and study it quietly.

"You alright?" he finally asks.

"I'm just fine," I assure him with a smile.

"Good," he replies with a wink. "I sure am glad."

I ask Angie for another coffee to go and offer to pay for breakfast. However, Joseph refuses to allow it.

"I'll take the bill, Miss Angie," he says with a nod when she comes to clear the table.

"You got it, sweetie!" She calls over her shoulder as she carries the plates through the swinging saloon doors and into the kitchen.

Outside in the parking lot, the sun warms my face as I look up at Joseph. "I seem to have gotten a bit of a second wind," I say, stirring my coffee with the plastic straw.

"Well, I think you should go home and get some rest," Joseph advises. "You've been through a lot in the past twenty-four hours."

"I have," I agree. "It has been the wildest of rides, for sure."

Even as I say the words, I find I'm actually grateful for that ride. I feel a transformation taking place within my spirit in light of the events that have penetrated my life lately.

"Are you headed for home, now?" Joseph asks.

"Almost. I have one more item of business to take care of first," I reply before taking a sip of the hot coffee.

"I'm not even going to ask." He chuckles.

"Just promise you'll get some rest. Please?"

"Oh, I promise. Don't you worry," I assure him. "Just one last thing I have to do."

He takes me in a gentle embrace. "Alright. Well, be careful," he says, as he combs through my unbrushed hair with his fingertips.

"I will," I promise, leaning further into him. With my head on his chest, I can hear his heart drumming rapidly.

"Call me when you get up this evening," I say, standing up straight and looking up to meet his gaze.

"First thing," he says, smiling.

He opens my car door for me and holds it open as I slide in and start the engine.

"See you tomorrow," he says before shutting the car door.

"Bye," I wave through the window before backing out of the parking space and heading back down the highway toward the sunrise.

SEVENTEEN
PSALM 91:4

As soon as Dill hears my key in the doorknob, he begins whining and pawing ferociously at the door.

"I know, I know. I'm coming, Dill!"

Poor guy probably wonders what happened to me last night. I don't think I've ever left him alone all night. It was absolutely unintentional, of course.

"Aw, hey buddy!" I squat to greet him properly as he covers my face in slobbery kisses and nearly knocks me onto my behind. I give him a good scratch on both ears and kiss the top of his soft, warm head before rising to my feet. The second my arm stretches out for the leash, he sits down expectantly at my feet.

"Poor Dill," I say as he sniffs for a spot to relieve himself. "Have you been alone all night?"

After he does his business, he runs back to me for praise and then immediately retreats to the house for his Milk Bone.

"We've got a little trip to make this morning, Dill," I say cheerfully as he pulls me through the garage.

Inside, I heave a cardboard box from the nearest stack and shove it into my back seat. Then, I grab another, and before I know it my back seat is full of boxes again.

"Might as well take a load, since we're going that way," I sing to Dill as he crunches into his dog biscuit.

Once I'm satisfied with the amount of things I've managed to squeeze into the car, I grab Dill's leash and turn the lock on the inside of the doorknob.

"Wanna go for a ride, Dill?" I ask enthusiastically.

At this, he bolts right past me and out to the garage, where he stands patiently beside my car and waits for me to open the door, still licking his lips.

"Alright, I'm coming," I call as I round the back of the car and let him hop into the passenger seat.

On the highway heading toward the farmhouse, I sip my lukewarm coffee and switch on the local pop radio station. I have to stay awake, just a while longer.

"You want to see your new house, Dill?" I ask excitedly. His ears perk up.

"We're almost there," I sing as we wind our way down the long curvy road.

As we finally pull into the driveway, I feel a peculiar sense of peace as I imagine Addie outside in the herb bed, carefully tending her seedlings. Or, marching out to the barn with her milk bucket in hand, calling for Ginger. I don't think I'll ever stop seeing her here.

Once we come to a stop in the front yard, I hook Dill's leash to him before letting him out of the car.

"You've got lots of room to run and lots of things to sniff, here," I tell him. "But you have to wear the leash today. I can't have you getting lost."

I let Dill get acquainted with the exterior of his soon-to-be home, while I follow behind him, admiring every part of it like I'm seeing it for the first time. In a way, I am.

We walk around inside the empty old barn, kicking up dust as with every stride. Dill seems to pick up the remnants of the farm animals' scent, as he walks with his nose to the red dirt floor.

Once we've made a giant circle around the property, taking in the scents and the scenes, I coax him back toward the house.

"Come on," I say, tugging at his leash. "We have to go in the house."

He happily comes along with me, up the driveway and toward the house. Once we reach the front steps, he bounds up them and then sits and waits by the door while I unlock it and push it open with a loud creak.

Inside, Dill pads across the hardwoods, looking around curiously at the home that stands empty other than the tower of boxes that Joseph and I stacked in the middle of the living room.

Though it is vacant, it remains warm and inviting. I can imagine Addie in the kitchen just off the living room, kneading sourdough bread or straining fresh milk. I marvel at the thought of all the hours she spent in this very space. She must've walked across these scuffed wooden floors thousands of times, tending to the home she created and preparing nourishment for the mothers she cared so much for.

"Come, Dill," I call as I cross the room. I look up the towering staircase and take one step at a time, holding onto the slick wooden railing, my mind focused on the purpose of my visit.

Dill and I reach the top step and I lead him gently to the hall closet, between the two bedrooms. I grasp the ivory doorknob and turn it, as I inhale the scent of old books and linens.

I reach into the darkness for the chain that's hanging from the light bulb. I pull it and the small empty closet becomes illuminated with a warm glow. I hang Dill's leash on the doorknob of the closet and kneel to the floor.

On my knees, I run my hands along the worn wooden planks. I press down and jiggle them a bit. Finally, I feel the one that's loose. I try to pry the floor plank up with my fingernail, but to no avail. Reaching into my back pocket, I pull my keys out.

Sliding my slender house key between the groove separating the two flat pieces of wood, I pry the loose board from the floor, and it pops out easily. I remove it from the floor where it's blended perfectly with the others, revealing a dark hole underneath.

I can't see anything down there. Illuminating my phone's screen, I hold it over the opening in the closet's floor. Tilting the light around at an angle, I lean forward and crane my neck so that I'm hovering directly over the hole.

There, lying just to the left, I see them. A whole stack of them. Reaching into the cool dark vault of sorts, I retrieve the cold, dusty books.

Holding them up in admiration, I count six of them in total. Six journals chocked full of Addie's deepest thoughts and unintentional offerings. Among the other worn journals, I take notice of the sea turtle and the butterfly printed covers that Addie had mentioned. Maybe I'll save those two for last.

Falling back into a sitting position on the closet floor, I take the stack of treasures against my chest in an embrace, resting my chin on them.

"Thank you, Addie," I whisper.

"For providing hope, healing, and now an everlasting and joyous gift in this home. I'll never leave this place, and I'll never forget you," I promise, as another tear slowly trickles down my cheek. I wonder how I've got any tears left in me.

Wiping my face, I turn around to see that Dill is sitting quietly and calmly, waiting for whatever's next.

In the same moment that I stand from the floor, the stack of precious books cradled in my right arm, Dill and I both hear a sound. It sounds like the beeping of a large truck backing up the driveway.

Dill's ears perk and he cocks his head. I quickly unhook his leash from the doorknob and we head back down the stairs toward the sound. The nearest neighbors aren't even within earshot, so I wonder who it could be.

Once in the living room, I can see through the big window that it's a delivery truck.

Dill and I walk out onto the porch, my grip tight on the leather leash. A large husky man wearing a worn-out ball cap and a sleeveless shirt exits the truck and approaches the porch. He walks stiffly, as if he's been driving the truck for a long time.

"Hi. Can I help you?" I ask.

"I've got a couch I'm supposed to deliver to nine oh nine. This the right place?" he asks as he points back at the truck with his thumb.

"Oh! Yeah, it is. I'd totally forgotten about that. Is today… What? *Monday*?" I ask, straining my mind. The last few days have all bled together.

"Yep. What door you want us to come through?" He asks, as the helper climbs out of the passenger seat of the truck.

What a wonderful personality this guy has, I notice.

"The front, please. I hope the door's wide enough," I say, looking back at opening.

"Yeah, me too," he comments dryly.

Dill and I walk across the porch and stand by the front windows as the two men haul the large plastic-covered sofa through the front door and into the house. Luckily, it was a perfect fit through the door.

"Thank you!" I yell as the two men walk back toward the delivery truck.

"No problem," the husky one calls back as he opens the truck door and hoists himself up into the driver's seat.

As the delivery truck speeds back down the dirt driveway toward the road, I take Dill and walk back into the house, where I lock the door behind us and unhook the leash from his raggedy old collar.

Just inside, the large piece of furniture sits along the front windows wrapped in clear plastic. I rip the tape that's holding the plastic taut and begin to remove it, revealing a tan corduroy sofa. It's much nicer than the one Dill and I are used to.

"Look, Dill!" I exclaim as he begins wagging his tail in excitement.

"You've got a new place to sleep. Come on," I say, sitting and patting the couch cushion next to me. He doesn't hesitate to jump up and make himself comfortable. He lays with his head resting on his paws, blending in almost perfectly with the color and texture of the new couch.

I crumple onto the soft, inviting cushion and relax next to him, resting my hands on his warm neck. Though none of our belongings are unpacked from the mountain of cardboard boxes in the center of the room, I've never felt more at home as I lay in the stillness of the quiet farmhouse. Suddenly, I have the divine realization that Addie's beautiful old table where I found her diary will soon be right back in the house where it started. I smile at the thought.

My body is blanketed with a peace unfathomable as my eyelids grow heavier with each passing second. Sitting on top of a cardboard box in front of me, are Addie's stack of diaries. They're the last thing I see before my eyes finally close, the soft weight of tranquility and a lifetime's wait for contentment, mine at last.

From the author:

Through the words written in Addie's diary, Blaire is able to find hope. From that hope, blossoms joy, and eventually...peace. Blaire leans on those comforting words in times of need. They lift her up, put her fears at ease, and even provide wisdom.

But the joy and hope that Blaire has found is soon stolen and replaced with fear, worry, and doubt. Though there was nothing to fear in the end, Blaire went through a period of great anxiety.

Just as Blaire finds hope, wisdom, and comfort in those words written by Addie, I find the same in God's Word. There's nothing that life brings, no trial so great, that cannot be soothed or solved by the wise counsel of the Almighty.

Though the enemy has, at times, sought to steal my joy and replace it with fears, doubts, and lies to cause worry, I know that when I lean on the words God promises and allow Him to be my comforter and healer, there really is nothing to fear in the end. And what's more... His words stand firm and unwavering forever!

Jesus said... "Come to Me, all you who labor and are heavy-laden, and I will give you rest."

www.ingramcontent.com/pod-product-compliance
Lightning Source LLC
Chambersburg PA
CBHW070423310726
48977CB00003B/808